Gulliver's Travels

GULLIVER'S TRAVELS

By Jonathan Swift

REVISED & SLIGHTLY ABRIDGED
FOR READERS OF OUR TIME

ILLUSTRATED BY *Aldren Watson*

Illustrated Junior Library

GROSSET & DUNLAP · PUBLISHERS
New York

ISBN: 0-448-05910-X (TRADE EDITION)

ISBN: 0-448-03247-3 (LIBRARY EDITION)

1971 PRINTING

THE SPECIAL CONTENTS OF THIS EDITION ARE
COPYRIGHT, 1947, BY GROSSET & DUNLAP, INC.

PRINTED IN THE UNITED STATES OF AMERICA BY

KINGSPORT PRESS, INC., KINGSPORT, TENN.

Library of Congress card number 47–27065

INTRODUCTION

GULLIVER'S TRAVELS was originally written as a political satire on English politics during the eighteenth century.

Jonathan Swift, the author, was born in Dublin, Ireland, in November, 1667. He studied at the University of Dublin, became a clergyman in the Church of England, and was appointed Dean of St. Patrick's, Dublin. This position gave him the title by which he is best known—Dean Swift.

Swift was deeply interested in politics, and by using the imaginary adventures of Gulliver he was able to criticize all that he considered unfair or unjust in the government of his country. The readers of his day understood the satire very well; to them, the imaginary people described in *Travels* represented groups of real people in British public life.

Later readers, uninterested in or unfamiliar with eighteenth century England, read—and today still read—the book as a wonderful adventure story.

The book was supposedly written by Lemuel Gulliver, a ship's captain from Nottinghamshire, England. He voyaged to some very queer countries, indeed. First he was shipwrecked on the coast of

Lilliput, a country of people only six inches tall. They called him a man-mountain. After amazing adventures among these little people, he sailed to Brobdingnag, land of giants, where he became the toy of the king and queen. On his next voyage he visited an island that floated in the air. The inhabitants of this island were so engrossed with mathematics and science that they had no time or thought for everyday affairs.

At this point he paid a visit to his family in England, but soon left again for more adventures. His last voyage took him to the country of the Houyhnhnms (the word sounds like the whinny of a horse). Here the government was carried on by horses, who were far superior to their apelike slaves, called Yahoos, who represented the human race.

Incidentally, Gulliver paid a short and rather unsatisfactory visit to Japan before finally settling in England, where he had a hard time readjusting himself to the customs and manners of his own people.

In order to make *Gulliver's Travels* suitable for inclusion in the Illustrated Junior Library, it was decided to omit Swift's long explanations of his own political philosophy, leaving the imaginative writing and the make-believe adventures of Gulliver.

CONTENTS

PART III ᕽᕽ *Voyages to Laputa and the Country of the Houyhnhnms*

Gulliver's Travels

PART I

A Voyage to Lilliput

CHAPTER 1

Gulliver Is Shipwrecked
and Made a Prisoner

MY FATHER had a small estate in Nottinghamshire. I was the third of five sons. He sent me to Emmanuel College in Cambridge at fourteen years of age; where I resided three years, and applied myself to my studies. But the charge of maintaining me (although I had a very scanty allowance) being too great for a narrow fortune, I was bound apprentice to Mr. James Bates, an eminent surgeon in London, with whom I continued four years. My father now and then sending me small sums of money, I laid them out in learning navigation, and other parts of mathematics useful to those who intend to travel, as I always believed it would be sometime or other my fortune to do. When I left Mr. Bates, I went down to my father; where, by the assistance of him and my

uncle John, and some other relations, I got forty
pounds, and a promise of thirty pounds a year to
maintain me at Leyden. There I studied physic two
years and seven months, knowing it would be useful
in long voyages.

Soon after my return from Leyden, I was recommended, by my good master Mr. Bates, to be surgeon to the *Swallow,* Captain Abraham Pannell
commander. With him I continued three years and
a half, making a voyage or two into the Levant, and
some other parts. When I came back, I resolved to
settle in London, in which Mr. Bates, my master, encouraged me, and by him I was recommended to
several patients. I took part of a small house in the
Old Jewry, and married Mary Burton, second
daughter to Mr. Edmund Burton, hosier, in New-
gate Street, with whom I received four hundred
pounds for a portion.

But, my good master Bates dying two years after,
and I having few friends, my business began to fail.
Having therefore consulted with my wife, and some
of my acquaintance, I determined to go again to sea.
I was surgeon successively in two ships, and made
several voyages, for six years, to the East and West
Indies, by which I got some addition to my fortune.
My hours of leisure I spent in reading the best au-
thors, ancient and modern, being always provided
with a good number of books; and when I was

ashore, in observing the manners and dispositions of the people, as well as learning their language, wherein I had a great facility by the strength of my memory.

The last of these voyages not proving very fortunate, I grew weary of the sea, and intended to stay at home with my wife and family. After three years' expectation that things would mend, I accepted an advantageous offer from Captain William Prichard, master of the *Antelope*, who was making a voyage to the South Sea. We set sail from Bristol May 4, 1699, and our voyage at first was very prosperous.

It would not be proper, for some reasons, to trouble the reader with the particulars of our adventures in those seas. Let it suffice to inform him that in our passage from thence to the East Indies we were driven by a violent storm to the northwest of Van Diemen's Land. Twelve of our crew were dead of immoderate labor and ill food, the rest were in a very weak condition. On the 5th of November, which was the beginning of summer in those parts, the weather being very hazy, the seamen spied a rock, within half a cable's length of the ship; but the wind was so strong that we were driven directly upon it, and immediately split.

Six of the crew, of whom I was one, having let down the boat into the sea, made a shift to get clear of the ship and the rock. We rowed by my computation about three leagues, till we were able to work no longer, being already spent with labor while we were in the ship. We therefore trusted ourselves to the mercy of the waves, and in about half an hour the boat was overset by a sudden flurry from the north. What became of my companions in the boat, as well as of those who escaped on the rock or were left in the vessel, I cannot tell; but conclude they were all lost.

For my own part, I swam as fortune directed me and was pushed forward by wind and tide. I often let my legs drop, and could feel no bottom. But when I was almost gone, and able to struggle no longer, I found myself within my depth; and by this time the storm was much abated. The declivity was so small that I walked near a mile before I got to the shore, which I conjectured was about eight o'clock in the evening. I then advanced forward near half a mile, but could not discover any sign of houses or inhabitants; at least I was in so weak a condition that I did not observe them. I was extremely tired, and with that, and the heat of the weather, and about half a pint of brandy that I drank as I left the ship, I found myself much inclined to sleep. I lay down on the grass, which was very short and soft. There I slept sounder than ever I remember to have done in my life, and, as I reckoned, above nine hours.

When I awakened, it was just daylight. I attempted to rise, but was not able to stir. For, as I happened to lie on my back, I found my arms and legs were strongly fastened on each side to the ground; and my hair, which was long and thick, tied down in the same manner. I likewise felt several slender ligatures across my body, from my armpits to my thighs. I could only look upward; the sun be-

gan to grow hot, and the light offended my eyes. I
heard a confused noise about me, but in the posture
I lay could see nothing except the sky.

In a little time I felt something alive moving on
my left leg, which advancing gently forward over
my breast, came almost up to my chin. Bending my
eyes downward as much as I could, I perceived it to
be a human creature not six inches high, with a bow
and arrow in his hands and a quiver at his back. In
the meantime, I felt at least forty more of the same
kind following the first. I was in the utmost astonishment and roared so loud that they all ran back in a

fright; and some of them, as I was afterward told, were hurt with the falls they got by leaping from my sides upon the ground. However, they soon returned, and one of them, who ventured so far as to get a full sight of my face, lifting up his hands and eyes by way of admiration, cried out in a shrill but distinct voice, *Hekinah degul.* The others repeated the same words several times, but I then knew not what they meant.

I lay all this while, as the reader may believe, in great uneasiness. At length, struggling to get loose, I had the fortune to break the strings, and wrench out the pegs that fastened my left arm to the ground. By lifting it up to my face, I discovered the methods they had taken to bind me, and at the same time, with a violent pull, which gave me excessive pain, I a little loosened the strings that tied down my hair on the left side, so that I was just able to turn my head about two inches. But the creatures ran off a second time, before I could seize them; whereupon there was a great shout in a very shrill accent.

After it ceased, I heard one of them cry aloud, *Tolgo phonac,* and in an instant I felt above a hundred arrows discharged on my left hand, which pricked me like so many needles; and besides they shot another flight into the air, as we do bombs in Europe, whereof many, I suppose, fell on my body (though I felt them not) and some on my face, which I immediately covered with my left hand. When this shower of arrows was over, I fell a-groaning with grief and pain. Then as I strove again to get loose, they discharged another volley larger than the first, and some of them attempted with spears to stick me in the sides; but, by good luck, I had on me a buff jerkin, which they could not pierce.

I thought it the most prudent method to lie still, and my design was to continue so till night, when, my left hand being already loose, I could easily free myself. As for the inhabitants, I had reason to believe I might be a match for the greatest armies they could bring against me, if they were all of the same size with him that I saw. But fortune disposed otherwise of me.

When the people observed I was quiet, they discharged no more arrows; but, by the noise I heard, I knew their numbers increased. About four yards from me, over against my right ear, I heard a knocking for above an hour, like that of people at work. When I turned my head that way, as well as the pegs and strings would permit me, I saw a stage erected, about a foot and a half from the ground, capable of holding four of the inhabitants, with two or three ladders to mount it: from whence one of them, who seemed to be a person of quality, made me a long speech, whereof I understood not one syllable. But I should have mentioned that, before the principal person began his oration, he cried out three times, *Langro dehul san* (these words and the former were afterward repeated and explained to me).

Whereupon immediately about fifty of the inhabitants came, and cut the strings that fastened the left side of my head, which gave me the liberty of turning it to the right and of observing the person and gesture of him that was to speak. He appeared to be of a middle age, and taller than any of the other three who attended him, whereof one was a page that held up his train, and seemed to be somewhat longer than my middle finger. The other two stood one on each side to support him. He acted every part of an orator, and I could observe many periods of threatenings, and others of promises, pity, and kind·· ness. I answered in a few words, but in the most sub· missive manner, lifting up my left hand and both my eyes to the sun, as calling him for a witness. I was almost famished with hunger, having not eaten a morsel for some hours before I left the ship. Indeed, I found the demands of nature so strong upon me that I could not forbear showing my impatience by putting my finger frequently on my mouth, to signify that I wanted food.

The *hurgo* (for so they call a great lord, as I afterward learned) understood me very well. He descended from the stage, and commanded that several ladders should be applied to my sides, on which

above a hundred of the inhabitants mounted. They
walked toward my mouth, laden with baskets full of
meat, which had been provided, and sent thither by
the King's orders, upon the first intelligence he received of me. I observed there was the flesh of several animals, but could not distinguish them by the
taste. There were shoulders, legs, and loins, shaped
like those of mutton, and very well dressed, but
smaller than the wings of a lark. I ate them by two or
three at a mouthful, and took three loaves at a time,
about the bigness of musket bullets. They supplied
me as they could, showing a thousand marks of
wonder and astonishment at my bulk and appetite.

I then made another sign that I wanted drink.
They found by my eating that a small quantity
would not suffice me. Being a most ingenious people,
they slung up with great dexterity one of their largest
hogsheads, then rolled it toward my hand, and beat
out the top. I drank it off at a draught, which I might
well do, for it did not hold half a pint, and tasted like
a small wine of Burgundy, but much more delicious.
They brought me a second hogshead, which I drank
in the same manner, and made signs for more, but
they had none to give me. When I had performed
these wonders, they shouted for joy, and danced
upon my breast, repeating several times as they did
at first, *Hekinah degul*. They made me a sign that I
should throw down the two hogsheads, but first

warning the people below to stand out of the way, crying aloud, *Borach mivola.* When they saw the vessels in the air, there was a universal shout of *Hekinah degul.*

I confess I was often tempted, while they were passing backward and forward on my body, to seize forty or fifty of the first that came in my reach, and dash them against the ground. But the remembrance of what I had felt, which probably might not be the worst they could do, and the promise of honor I made them soon drove out these imaginations. Besides, I now considered myself as bound by the laws of hospitality to a people who had treated me with so much expense and magnificence. However, in my thoughts I could not sufficiently wonder at the intrepidity of these diminutive mortals, who dared venture to mount and walk upon my body, while one of my hands was at liberty, without trembling at the very sight of so prodigious a creature as I must appear to them.

After some time, there appeared before me a person of high rank from his Imperial Majesty. His Excellency, having mounted on the small of my right leg, advanced forward up to my face, with about a dozen of his retinue. Having produced his credentials he spoke for about ten minutes, often pointing toward the capital city, whither it was agreed by his Majesty in council that I must be conveyed. I an-

swered in few words, but to no purpose, and made a
sign with my hand that was loose, putting it to the
other and then to my own head and body, to signify
that I desired my liberty.

It appeared that he understood me well enough,
for he shook his head by way of disapprobation, and
held his hand in a posture to show that I must be
carried as a prisoner. However, he made other signs
to let me understand that I should have meat and
drink enough, and very good treatment. Whereupon
I once more thought of attempting to break my
bonds. But again, when I felt the smart of their arrows upon my face and hands, which were all in
blisters, and many of the darts still sticking in them,
and observing likewise that the number of my enemies increased, I gave tokens to let them know that
they might do with me what they pleased. Upon this
the *hurgo* and his train withdrew with much civility
and cheerful countenances.

Before this, they had daubed my face and both
my hands with a sort of ointment very pleasant
to the smell, which in a few minutes removed all
the smart of their arrows. These circumstances,
added to the refreshment I had received by their
victuals and drink, which were very nourishing, disposed me to sleep. I slept about eight hours.

It seems that upon the first moment I was discovered sleeping on the ground after my landing,

the Emperor had early notice of it by an express. It was determined in council that I should be tied in the manner I have related, that plenty of meat and drink should be sent me, and a machine prepared to carry me to the capital city.

These people are most excellent mathematicians, having been encouraged by the Emperor, who is a renowned patron of learning. This prince has several machines fixed on wheels for the carriage of trees and other great weights. He often builds his largest men-of-war, whereof some are nine feet long, in the woods where the timber grows, and has them carried on these engines three or four hundred yards to the sea. Five hundred carpenters and engineers were immediately set at work to prepare the greatest engine they had. It was a frame of wood raised three inches from the ground, about seven feet long and four wide, moving upon twenty-two wheels.

This engine was brought parallel to me as I lay. But the principal difficulty was to raise and place me in this vehicle. Eighty poles, each of one foot high, were erected for this purpose, and very strong cords of the bigness of packthread were fastened by hooks to many bandages, which the workmen had girt round my neck, my hands, my body, and my legs. Nine hundred of the strongest men were employed to draw up these cords by many pulleys fastened on the poles, and thus, in less than three hours, I was

raised and slung into the engine, and there tied fast.
All this I was told, for while the whole operation was
performing, I lay in a profound sleep. Fifteen hundred of the Emperor's largest horses, each about four
inches and a half high, were employed to draw me
toward the metropolis, which was half a mile distant.

About four hours after we began our journey, I
awaked by a very ridiculous accident. The carriage
being stopped awhile to adjust something that was
out of order, two or three of the young natives had
the curiosity to see how I looked when I was asleep.
They climbed up into the engine, and advancing

very softly to my face, one of them put the sharp end of his half-pike a good way up into my left nostril, which tickled my nose like a straw, and made me sneeze violently: whereupon they stole off unperceived, and it was three weeks before I knew the cause of my awaking so suddenly.

We made a long march the remaining part of that day, and rested at night with five hundred guards on each side of me, half with torches, and half with bows and arrows, ready to shoot me if I should offer to stir. The next morning at sunrise we continued our march, and arrived within two hundred yards of the city gates about noon. The Emperor and all his court came out to meet us; but his great officers would by no means suffer his Majesty to endanger his person by mounting on my body.

At the place where the carriage stopped, there stood an ancient temple, esteemed to be the largest in the whole kingdom, and in this edifice it was determined I should lodge. The great gate fronting to the north was about four feet high, and almost two feet wide, through which I could easily creep. On each side of the gate was a small window not above six inches from the ground. Into that on the left side, the King's smiths conveyed fourscore and eleven chains, like those that hang to a lady's watch in Europe, and almost as large. These were locked to my left leg with six and thirty padlocks.

Over against this temple, on the other side of the great highway, at twenty feet distance, there was a turret at least five feet high. Here the Emperor ascended with many principal lords of his court, to have an opportunity of viewing me, as I was told, for I could not see them. It was reckoned that above a hundred thousand inhabitants came out of the town upon the same errand. And in spite of my guards, I believe there could not be fewer than ten thousand, at several times, who mounted upon my body by the help of ladders. But a proclamation was soon issued to forbid it upon pain of death.

When the workmen found it was impossible for me to break loose, they cut all the strings that bound me; whereupon I rose up with as melancholy a disposition as ever I had in my life. But the noise and astonishment of the people at seeing me rise and walk are not to be expressed. The chains that held my left leg were about two yards long, and gave me not only the liberty of walking backward and forward in a semicircle, but, being fixed within four inches of the gate, allowed me to creep in, and lie at my full length in the temple.

CHAPTER 2

The Emperor of Lilliput

WHEN I FOUND myself on my feet, I looked about me, and must confess I never beheld a more entertaining prospect. The country round appeared like a continued garden, and the enclosed fields, which were generally forty feet square, resembled so many beds of flowers. These fields were intermingled with woods of half a stang, and the tallest trees, as I could judge, appeared to be seven feet high. I viewed the town on my left hand, which looked like the painted scene of a city in a theater.

The Emperor was already descended from the tower, and advancing on horseback toward me, which had like to have cost him dear. The beast, though very well trained, yet wholly unused to such a sight, which appeared as if a mountain moved before him, reared up on his hinder feet: but that prince, who is an excellent horseman, kept his seat, till his attendants ran in and held the bridle, while his Majesty had time to dismount. When he alighted, he surveyed me round with great admiration, but kept without the length of my chain.

He ordered his cooks and butlers, who were already prepared, to give me victuals and drink, which they pushed forward in a sort of vehicle upon wheels till I could reach them. I took these vehicles, and soon emptied them all. Twenty of them were filled with meat, and ten with liquor. Each of the former afforded me two or three good mouthfuls, and I emptied the liquor of ten vessels, which was contained in earthen vials, into one vehicle, drinking it off at a draught; and so I did with the rest.

The Empress and young princes of the blood of both sexes, attended by many ladies, sat at some distance in their chairs. But upon the accident that happened to the Emperor's horse, they alighted, and came near his person, which I am now going to describe.[1] He was taller by almost the breadth of my nail than any of his court, which alone was enough to strike an awe into the beholders. His features were strong and masculine, with an Austrian lip and arched nose, his complexion olive, his countenance erect, his body and limbs well proportioned, all his motions graceful, and his deportment majestic. He

[1] This could be a portrait of George I.

was then past his prime, being twenty-eight years and three-quarters old, of which he had reigned about seven, in great felicity, and generally victorious.

For the better convenience of beholding him, I lay on my side, so that my face was parallel to his, and he stood but three yards off. However, I have had him since many times in my hand, and therefore cannot be deceived in the description. His dress was very plain and simple, and the fashion of it between the Asiatic and the European. But he had on his head a light helmet of gold, adorned with jewels, and a plume on the crest. He held his sword drawn in his hand, to defend himself, if I should happen to break loose. It was almost three inches long, the hilt and scabbard were gold enriched with diamonds. His voice was shrill, but very clear and articulate, and I could distinctly hear it when I stood up. The ladies and courtiers were all most magnificently clad, so that the spot they stood upon seemed to resemble a petticoat spread on the ground, embroidered with figures of gold and silver.

His Imperial Majesty spoke often to me, and I returned answers, but neither of us could understand a syllable. There were several of his priests and lawyers present (as I conjectured by their habits) who were commanded to address themselves to me. I spoke to them in as many languages as I had the least

They saw me take out my penknife

[SEE PAGE 21]

smattering of, which were High and Low Dutch, Latin, French, Spanish, Italian, and Lingua Franca; but all to no purpose.

After about two hours the court retired, and I was left with a strong guard, to prevent the impertinence and probably the malice of the rabble, who were very impatient to crowd about me as near as they dared. Some of them had the impudence to shoot their arrows at me as I sat on the ground by the door of my house, whereof one very narrowly missed my left eye. But the colonel ordered six of the ring-leaders to be seized, and thought no punishment so proper as to deliver them bound into my hands. Some of his soldiers accordingly did, pushing them forward with the butt ends of their pikes into my reach. I took them all in my right hand, put five of them into my coat pocket, and as to the sixth, I made a countenance as if I would eat him alive. The poor man squalled terribly, and the colonel and his officers were in much pain, especially when they saw me take out my penknife. But I soon put them out of fear; for immediately cutting the strings he was bound with, I set him gently on the ground, and away he ran. I treated the rest in the same manner, taking them one by one out of my pocket, and I observed both the soldiers and people were highly pleased of my clemency.

Toward night I with some difficulty got into my

house, where I lay on the ground, and continued to do so about a fortnight; during which time the Emperor gave orders to have a bed prepared for me. Six hundred beds of the common measure were brought in carriages, and worked up in my house. A hundred and fifty of their beds sewn together made up the breadth and length, and these were four double, which however kept me but very indifferently from the hardness of the floor, that was of smooth stone. By the same computation they provided me with sheets, blankets, and coverlets, tolerable enough for one who had been so long inured to hardships.

As the news of my arrival spread through the kingdom, it brought prodigious numbers of rich, idle and curious people to see me; so that the villages were almost emptied. Great neglect of tillage and household affairs must have ensued, if his Imperial Majesty had not provided, by several proclamations and orders of state, against this inconvenience. He directed that those who had already beheld me should return home, and not presume to come within fifty yards of my house without license from court, whereby the secretaries of state got considerable fees.

In the meantime, the Emperor held frequent councils to debate what course should be taken with me. I was afterward assured by a particular friend, a person of great quality, that the court was under many difficulties concerning me. They apprehended my breaking loose, that my diet would be very expensive, and might cause a famine. Sometimes they determined to starve me, or at least to shoot me in the face and hands with poisoned arrows, which would soon dispatch me. But again they considered that the stench of so large a carcass might produce a plague in the metropolis, and probably spread through the whole kingdom.

In the midst of these consultations, several army officers went to the door of the great council chamber. Two of them being admitted, they gave an account of my behavior to the six criminals above mentioned, which made so favorable an impression in the breast of his Majesty and the whole board in my behalf that an imperial commission was issued out, obliging all the villages nine hundred yards round the city, to deliver every morning six beeves, forty sheep, and other victuals for my sustenance; together with a proportionable quantity of bread, and wine, and other liquors for the due payment of which his Majesty gave assignments upon his treasury. For this prince lives chiefly upon his own demesnes, seldom raising any subsidies upon his subjects.

An establishment was also made of six hundred persons to be my domestics, who had board-wages allowed for their maintenance, and tents built for them very conveniently on each side of my door. It was likewise ordered that three hundred tailors should make me a suit of clothes after the fashion of the country; that six of his Majesty's greatest scholars should be employed to instruct me in their language; and, lastly, that the Emperor's horses, and those of the nobility, and troops of guards, should be frequently exercised in my sight, to accustom themselves to me.

All these orders were duly put in execution, and in about three weeks I made great progress in learning their language; during which time the Emperor frequently honored me with his visits, and was pleased to assist my masters in teaching me.

We began already to converse together in some fashion; and the first words I learned were to express my desire that he would please give me my liberty, which I every day repeated on my knees. His answer, as I could apprehend it, was that this must be a work of time, not to be thought on without the advice of his council, and that first I must *Lumos kelmin pesso desmar lon Emposo;* that is, swear a peace with him and his kingdom. Meanwhile, I should be used with all kindness, and he advised me to acquire, by my patience and discreet behavior, the good opinion of himself and his subjects.

He desired I would not take it ill if he gave orders to certain proper officers to search me; for probably I might carry about me several weapons, which must needs be dangerous things, if they answered the bulk of so prodigious a person. I said his Majesty should be satisfied, for I was ready to strip myself, and turn out my pockets before him. This I delivered part in words, and part in signs. He replied, that by the laws of the kingdom I must be searched by two of his officers. He said that he knew this could not be done without my consent and assistance; but that he had so good an opinion of my generosity and justice as to trust their persons in my hands. Whatever they took from me should be returned when I left the country, or paid for at the rate which I would set upon them.

I took up the two officers in my hands, put them into my coat pockets, and then into every other pocket about me, except my two fobs, and another secret pocket I had no mind should be searched, wherein I had some little necessaries that were of no consequence to any but myself. In one of my fobs there was a silver watch, and in the other a small quantity of gold in a purse. These gentlemen, having pen, ink, and paper about them, made an exact inventory of everything they saw; and when they were through, desired I would set them down, that they might deliver it to the Emperor. This inventory I afterward translated into English, and is word for word as follows:

In the right coat pocket of the Great Man-Mountain after the strictest search, we found only one great piece of coarse cloth, large enough to be a foot cloth for your Majesty's chief room of state. In the left pocket we saw a huge silver chest, with a cover of the same metal, which we the searchers were not able to lift. We desired it should be opened, and one of us stepping into it, found himself up to the mid-leg in a sort of dust, some part whereof flying up to our faces, set us both sneezing for several times together.

In his right waistcoat pocket we found a prodigious bundle of white thin substances, folded one over another, about the bigness of three men, tied with a strong cable, and marked with black figures; which we humbly conceive to be writings, every let-

ter almost half as large as the palm of our hands. In the left there was a sort of engine, from the back of which were extended twenty long poles, resembling the palisados before your Majesty's court; wherewith we conjecture the Man-Mountain combs his head, for we did not always trouble him with questions, because we found it a great difficulty to make him understand us.

In the large pocket on the right side of his breeches we saw a hollow pillar of iron, about the length of a man, fastened to a strong piece of timber, larger than the pillar; and upon one side of the pillar were huge pieces of iron sticking out, cut into strange figures, which we know not what to make of. In the left pocket, another engine of the same kind.

In the smaller pocket on the right side were several round flat pieces of white and red metal, of different bulk. Some of the white, which seemed to be silver, were so large and heavy that my comrade and I could hardly lift them. In the left pocket were two black pillars irregularly shaped. We could not, without difficulty, reach the top of them as we stood at the bottom of his pocket. One of them was covered, and seemed all of a piece. But at the upper end of the other, there appeared a white round substance, about twice the bigness of our heads. Within each of these was enclosed a prodigious plate of steel; which, by our orders, we obliged him to show

us, because we apprehended they might be dangerous engines. He took them out of their cases, and
told us that in his own country his practice was to
shave his beard with one of these, and to cut his meat
with the other.

There were two pockets which we could not enter: these he called his fobs. They were two large
slits cut into the top of his breeches, but squeezed
close by the pressure of his belly.

Out of the right fob hung a great silver chain, with
a wonderful kind of engine at the bottom. We directed him to draw out whatever was fastened to
that chain; which appeared to be a globe, half silver,
and half of some transparent metal. On the transparent side we saw certain strange figures circularly
drawn, and thought we could touch them, till we
found our fingers stopped by that lucid substance.
He put this engine to our ears, which made an inces-
sant noise like that of a watermill. We conjecture it
is either some unknown animal, or the god that he
worships; but we are more inclined to the latter
opinion, because he assured us that he seldom did
anything without consulting it. He called it his or-
acle, and said it pointed out the time for every action
of his life.

From the left fob he took out a net almost large
enough for a fisherman, but contrived to open and
shut like a purse and serve him for the same use. We

found therein several massy pieces of yellow metal, which, if they be real gold, must be of immense value.

Having thus, in obedience to your Majesty's commands, diligently searched all his pockets, we observed a girdle about his waist made of the hide of some prodigious animal; from which, on the left side, hung a sword of the length of five men; and on the right, a bag or pouch divided into two cells, each cell capable of holding three of your Majesty's subjects. In one of these cells were several globes or balls of a most ponderous metal, about the bigness of our heads, and requiring a strong hand to lift them. The other cell contained a heap of certain black grains, but of no great bulk or weight, for we could hold above fifty of them in the palms of our hands.

This is an exact inventory of what we found about the body of the Man-Mountain, who used us with great civility and due respect to your Majesty's commission. Signed and sealed on the fourth day of the eighty-ninth moon of your Majesty's auspicious reign.

CLEFREN FRELOCK
MARSI FRELOCK

When this inventory was read over to the Emperor, he directed me, although in very gentle terms, to deliver up the several particulars. He first called for my scimitar, which I took out, scabbard and all.

In the meantime he ordered three thousand of his
choicest troops to surround me at a distance, with
their bows and arrows just ready to discharge: but I
did not observe it, for my eyes were wholly fixed
upon his Majesty.

He then desired me to draw my scimitar, which, although it had got some rust by the sea water, was in most parts exceeding bright. I did so, and immediately all the troops gave a shout between terror and surprise; for the sun shone clear, and the reflection dazzled their eyes as I waved the scimitar to and fro in my hand. His Majesty, who is a most magnanimous prince, was less daunted than I could expect. He ordered me to return it into the scabbard, and cast it on the ground as gently as I could, about six feet from the end of my chain.

The next thing he demanded was one of the hollow iron pillars, by which he meant my pocket pistols. I drew it out, and at his desire, as well as I could, expressed to him the use of it. Charging it only with powder, I first cautioned the Emperor not to be afraid, and then I let it off in the air. The astonishment here was much greater than at the sight of my scimitar. Hundreds fell down as if they had been struck dead; and even the Emperor, although he stood his ground, could not recover himself in some time.

I delivered up both my pistols in the same manner as I had done my scimitar, and then my pouch of powder and bullets; begging him that the former might be kept from the fire, for it would kindle with the smallest spark, and blow his Imperial palace into the air. I likewise delivered up my watch, which the

Emperor was very curious to see, and commanded two of his tallest yeomen of the guards to bear it on a pole upon their shoulders, as draymen in England do a barrel of ale. He was amazed at the continual noise it made, and the motion of the minute hand, which he could easily discern. He asked the opinions of his learned men about him, which were various and remote, as the reader may well imagine; although indeed I could not very perfectly understand them. I then gave up my silver and copper money, my purse with nine large pieces of gold, and some smaller ones; my knife and razor, my comb and silver snuffbox, my handkerchief and journal book. My scimitar, pistols, and pouch were conveyed in carriages to his Majesty's stores; but the rest of my goods were returned me.

I had, as I before observed, one private pocket which escaped their search, wherein there was a pair of spectacles (which I sometimes use for the weakness of my eyes), a pocket perspective, and several other little conveniences. These being of no consequence to the Emperor, I did not think myself bound in honor to discover, and I apprehended they might be lost or spoiled if I ventured them out of my possession.

CHAPTER 3

Gulliver at the Court

of Lilliput

MY GENTLENESS and good behavior had gained so far on the Emperor and his court, and indeed upon the army and people in general, that I began to conceive hopes of getting my liberty in a short time. I took all possible methods to cultivate this favorable disposition. The natives came by degrees to be less apprehensive of any danger from me. I would sometimes lie down, and let five or six of them dance on my hand. And at last the boys and girls would venture to come and play at hide and seek in my hair. I had now made good progress in understanding and speaking their language. The Emperor had a mind one day to entertain me with several of the country shows, wherein they exceeded all nations I have known, for both dexterity and magnificence. I was diverted with none so much as that of the rope dancers, performed upon a slender white thread, extended about two feet, and twelve inches from the ground.

This diversion is practiced only by those persons who are candidates for great employments and high favors at court. They are trained in this art from their youth, and are not always of noble birth or liberal education. When a great office is vacant either by death or disgrace, five or six of those candidates petition the Emperor to entertain his Majesty and the court with a dance on the rope, and whoever jumps the highest without falling succeeds in the office. Very often the chief ministers themselves are commanded to show their skill, and to convince the Emperor that they have not lost their faculty.[1] Flimnap, the Treasurer, is allowed to cut a caper on the straight rope, at least an inch higher than any other lord in the whole empire. I have seen him do the summerset several times together upon a trencher fixed on the rope, which is no thicker than a common packthread in England. My friend Reldresal, Principal Secretary for Private Affairs, is, in my opinion, if I am not partial, the second after the Treasurer; the rest of the great officers are much upon a par.

These diversions are often attended with fatal accidents. I myself have seen two or three candidates break a limb. But the danger is much greater when

[1] This makes fun of politicians' efforts to secure office.

the ministers themselves are commanded to show
their dexterity; for they strain so far that there is
hardly one of them who has not received a fall, and
some of them two or three. I was assured that a year
or two before my arrival Flimnap would have in-
evitably broken his neck, if one of the King's cush-
ions, that accidentally lay on the ground, had not
weakened the force of his fall.

There is likewise another diversion, which is
shown only before the Emperor and Empress and
the first minister upon particular occasions. The Emperor lays on the table three fine silken threads of six
inches long. One is blue, the other red, and the third
green. These threads are proposed as prizes for those
persons whom the Emperor has a mind to distinguish by a peculiar mark of his favor.[1] The ceremony
is performed in his Majesty's great chamber of state,
where the candidates are to undergo a trial of dexterity very different from the former, and such as I
have not observed the least resemblance of in any
other country of the Old or the New World. The Emperor holds a stick in his hands, both ends parallel
to the horizon, while the candidates, advancing one
by one, sometimes leap over the stick, sometimes
creep under it backward and forward several times,
according as the stick is advanced or depressed.
Sometimes the Emperor holds one end of the stick,

[1] Reference is to the three orders of British knighthood.

and his first minister the other. Sometimes the minister has it entirely to himself. Whoever performs his part with most agility, and holds out the longest in leaping and creeping, is rewarded with the blue-colored silk. The red is given to the next, and the green to the third, which they all wear girt twice round about the middle. You see few great persons about this court who are not adorned with one of these girdles.

The horses of the army and those of the royal stables, having been daily led before me, were no longer shy, but would come up to my very feet without starting. The riders would leap them over my hand as I held it on the ground, and one of the Emperor's huntsmen, upon a large courser, took my

foot, shoe and all; which was indeed a prodigious leap. I had the good fortune to divert the Emperor one day after a very extraordinary manner. I desired he would order several sticks two feet high, and the thickness of an ordinary cane, to be brought me; whereupon his Majesty commanded the master of his woods to give directions accordingly. The next morning six woodmen arrived with as many carriages, drawn by eight horses each. I took nine of these sticks, and fixing them firmly in the ground in a quadrangular figure, two feet and a half square, I took four other sticks, and tied them parallel at each corner, about two feet from the ground. Then I fastened my handkerchief to the nine sticks that stood erect, and extended it on all sides till it was as tight as the top of a drum; and the four parallel sticks rising about five inches higher than the handkerchief served as ledges on each side. When I had finished my work, I desired the Emperor to let a troop of his best horse, twenty-four in number, come and exercise upon this plain. His Majesty approved of the proposal, and I took them up one by one in my hands, ready mounted and armed, with the proper officers to exercise them. As soon as they got into order, they divided into two parties, performed mock skirmishes, discharged blunt arrows, drew their swords, fled and pursued, attacked and retired, and in short discovered the best military discipline

I ever beheld. The parallel sticks secured them and their horses from falling over the stage. The Emperor was so much delighted that he ordered this entertainment to be repeated several days, and once was pleased to be lifted up and give the word of command. With great difficulty, he persuaded even the Empress herself to let me hold her in her close chair within two yards of the stage, from whence she was able to take a full view of the whole performance. It was my good fortune that no ill accident happened in these entertainments, only once a fiery horse that belonged to one of the captains pawing with his hoof struck a hole in my handkerchief, and his foot slipping, he overthrew his rider and himself. But I immediately relieved them both, and covering the hole with one hand, I set down the troop with the other, in the same manner as I took them up. The horse that fell was strained in the left shoulder, but the rider got no hurt, and I repaired my handkerchief as well as I could. However, I would not trust to the strength of it any more in such dangerous enterprises.

About two or three days before I was set at liberty, as I was entertaining the court with these feats, there arrived an express to inform his Majesty that some of his subjects riding near the place where I was first taken up had seen a great black substance lying on the ground, very oddly shaped, extending its edges

round as wide as his Majesty's bedchamber, and rising up in the middle as high as a man. It was no living creature, as they at first apprehended, for it lay
on the grass without motion, and some of them had
walked round it several times. By mounting upon
each other's shoulders, they had got to the top, which
was flat and even, and stamping upon it they found
it was hollow within. They humbly conceived it
might be something belonging to the Man-Mountain, and if his Majesty pleased, they would undertake to bring it with only five horses. I presently
knew what they meant, and was glad at heart to receive this intelligence. It seems upon my first reaching the shore after our shipwreck I was in such con-
fusion that before I came to the place where I went
to sleep, my hat, which I had fastened with a string
to my head while I was rowing, and had stuck on all
the time I was swimming, fell off after I came to
land. The string, as I conjecture, must have broken
by some accident which I never observed, but
thought my hat had been lost at sea. I entreated his
Imperial Majesty to give orders it might be brought
to me as soon as possible, describing to him the use
and the nature of it. The next day the wagoners arrived with it, but not in a very good condition. They
had bored two holes in the brim, within an inch and
a half of the edge, and fastened two hooks in the
holes; these hooks were tied by a long cord to the

harness, and thus my hat was dragged along for above half an English mile. But the ground in that country being extremely smooth and level, it received less damage than I expected.

I had sent so many memorials and petitions for my liberty, that his Majesty at length mentioned the matter, first in the cabinet, and then in a full council; where it was opposed by none except Skyresh Bolgolam, who was pleased, without any provocation, to be my mortal enemy. He was very much in his master's confidence, and a person well versed in affairs, but of a morose and sour complexion. However, he was at length persuaded to comply; but prevailed that the articles and conditions upon which I should be set free, and to which I must swear, should be drawn up by himself. These articles were brought to me by Skyresh Bolgolam in person, attended by two undersecretaries, and several persons of distinction. After they were read, I was demanded to swear to the performance of them; first in the manner of my own country, and afterward in the method prescribed by their laws; which was to hold my right foot in my left hand, to place the middle finger of my right hand on the crown of my head, and my thumb on the tip of my right ear. But because the reader may perhaps be curious to have some idea of the style and manner of expression peculiar to that people, as well as to know the articles upon which

I recovered my liberty, I have made a translation of
the whole instrument word for word, as near as I was
able, which I here offer to the public:

GOLBASTO MOMAREN EVLAME GURDILO SHEFIN
MULLY ULLY GUE, most mighty Emperor of Lilliput, delight and terror of the universe, whose dominions extend five thousand *blustrugs* (about twelve
miles in circumference) to the extremities of the
globe; monarch of all monarchs, taller than the sons
of men; whose feet press down to the center, and
whose head strikes against the sun; at whose nod the
princes of the earth shake their knees; pleasant as
the spring, comfortable as the summer, fruitful as
autumn, dreadful as winter His most sublime Majesty proposes to the Man-Mountain, lately arrived
to our celestial dominions, the following articles,
which by a solemn oath he shall be obliged to perform:

I. The Man-Mountain shall not depart from our
dominions without our license under our great seal.

II. He shall not presume to come into our metropolis without our express order; at which time the inhabitants shall have two hours' warning to keep
within their doors.

III. The said Man-Mountain shall confine his
walks to our principal highroads, and not offer to
walk or lie down in a meadow or field of corn.

IV. As he walks the said roads, he shall take the
utmost care not to trample upon the bodies of any of

our loving subjects, their horses, or carriages, nor take any of our said subjects into his hands, without their own consent.

V. If an express requires extraordinary dispatch, the Man-Mountain shall be obliged to carry in his pocket the messenger and horse a six days' journey once in every moon, and return the said messenger back (if so required) safe to our Imperial Presence.

VI. He shall be our ally against our enemies in the island of Blefuscu,[1] and do his utmost to destroy their fleet, which is now preparing to invade us.

VII. That the said Man-Mountain shall, at his times of leisure, be aiding and assisting to our workmen, in helping to raise certain great stones, toward covering the wall of the principal park, and other of our royal buildings.

VIII. That the said Man-Mountain shall, in two moons' time, deliver in an exact survey of the circumference of our dominions by a computation of his own paces round the coast.

Lastly, That upon his solemn oath to observe all the above articles, the said Man-Mountain shall have a daily allowance of meat and drink sufficient for the support of 1,728 of our subjects, with free access to our Royal Person, and other marks of our favor. Given at our palace at Belfaborac the twelfth day of the ninety-first moon of our reign.

I swore and subscribed to these articles with great

[1] Since Lilliput refers to England, this is probably France.

cheerfulness and content, although some of them were not so honorable as I could have wished; whereupon my chains were immediately unlocked, and I was at full liberty. The Emperor himself in person did me the honor to be by at the whole ceremony. I made my acknowledgments by prostrating myself at his Majesty's feet: but he commanded me to rise. And after many gracious expressions, he added that he hoped I should prove a useful servant, and well deserve all the favors he had already conferred upon me, or might do for the future.

CHAPTER 4

The Emperor's Palace and

His Principal Secretary

THE FIRST REQUEST I made after I had obtained my liberty was that I might have license to see Mildendo, the metropolis. This the Emperor easily granted me, but with a special charge to do no hurt either to the inhabitants or their houses. The people had notice by proclamation of my design to visit the town. The wall which encompassed it is two feet and a half high, and at least eleven inches broad, so that a coach and horses may be driven very safely round it; and it is flanked with strong towers at ten feet distance. I stepped over the great Western Gate, and passed very gently, and sidling through the two principal streets, only in my short waistcoat, for fear of damaging the roofs and eaves of the houses with the skirts of my coat.

I walked with the utmost circumspection, to avoid

treading on any stragglers that might remain in the streets, although the orders were very strict that all people should keep in their houses at their own peril. The garret windows and tops of houses were so crowded with spectators that I thought in all my travels I had not seen a more populous place. The city is an exact square, each side of the wall being five hundred feet long. The two great streets, which run cross and divide it into four quarters, are five feet wide. The lanes and alleys, which I could not enter, but only viewed them as I passed, are from twelve to eighteen inches. The town is capable of holding five hundred thousand souls. The houses are from three to five stories; the shops and markets well provided.

The Emperor's palace is in the center of the city, where the two great streets meet. It is enclosed by a wall two feet high, and twenty feet distant from the buildings. I had his Majesty's permission to step over this wall; and the space being so wide between that and the palace, I could easily view it on every side. The outward court is a square of forty feet, and includes two other courts. In the inmost are the royal apartments, which I was very desirous to see, but found it extremely difficult; for the great gates, from one square into another, were but eighteen inches high and seven inches wide. Now the buildings of the outer court were at least five feet high, and it was impossible for me to stride over them without infinite damage to the pile, though the walls were strongly built of hewn stone, and four inches thick.

At the same time the Emperor had a great desire that I should see the magnificence of his palace. But this I was not able to do till three days after, which I spent in cutting down with my knife some of the largest trees in the royal park, about a hundred yards distant from the city. Of these trees I made two stools, each about three feet high, and strong enough to bear my weight. The people having received notice a second time, I went again through the city to the palace with my two stools in my hands. When I came to the side of the outer court, I stood upon one stool, and took the other in my hand: this I lifted over the roof, and gently set it down on the space between the first and second court, which was eight feet wide. I then stepped over the buildings very conveniently from one stool to the other, and drew up the first after me with a hooked stick. By this contrivance I got into the inmost court. Lying down upon my side, I applied my face to the windows of the middle stories, which were left open on purpose, and discovered the most splendid apartments that can be imagined.

There I saw the Empress and the young princes, in their several lodgings, with their chief attendants about them. Her Imperial Majesty was pleased to smile very graciously upon me, and gave me out of the window her hand to kiss.

One morning, about a fortnight after I had obtained my liberty, Reldresal, Principal Secretary of Private Affairs, came to my house attended only by one servant. He ordered his coach to wait at a distance, and desired I would give him an hour's audience; which I readily consented to, on account of his quality and personal merits, as well as the many good offices he had done me during my solicitations at court. I offered to lie down, that he might the more conveniently reach my ear; but he chose rather to let me hold him in my hand during our conversation. He began with compliments on my liberty; said he might pretend to some merit in it: but added that, if it had not been for the present situation of things at court, perhaps I might not have obtained it so soon. "For," said he, "as flourishing a condition as we may appear to be in to foreigners, we labor under two mighty evils: a violent faction at home, and the danger of an invasion by a most potent enemy from abroad. As to the first, you are to understand that for above seventy moons past there have been two struggling parties in this empire, under the names of *Tramecksan* and *Slamecksan*, from the high and low heels on their shoes, by which they distinguish themselves. It is alleged, indeed, that the high heels are most agreeable to our ancient constitution. But how-

ever this be, his Majesty has determined to make use
of only low heels in the administration of the government and all offices in the gift of the Crown, as you
cannot but observe; and particularly, that his Majesty's Imperial heels are lower at least by a *drurr*
than any of his court (*drurr* is a measure about the
fourteenth part of an inch). The animosities between these two parties run so high that they will
neither eat nor drink, nor talk with each other.

"Now, in the midst of these domestic disquiets, we
are threatened with an invasion from the island of
Blefuscu, which is the other great empire of the universe, almost as large and powerful as this of his Majesty. For as to what we have heard you affirm, that
there are other kingdoms and states in the world inhabited by human creatures as large as yourself, our
philosophers are in much doubt and would rather
conjecture that you dropped from the moon, or one
of the stars; because it is certain that a hundred mortals of your bulk would, in a short time, destroy all
the fruits and cattle of his Majesty's dominions. Besides, our histories of six thousand moons make no
mention of any other regions than the two great empires of Lilliput and Blefuscu. Which two mighty
powers have, as I was going to tell you, been engaged in a most obstinate war for six and thirty
moons past.

"It began upon the following occasion: It is allowed on all hands that the primitive way of breaking eggs before we eat them was upon the larger end: but his present Majesty's grandfather, while he was a boy, going to eat an egg, and breaking it according to the ancient practice, happened to cut one of his fingers. Whereupon the Emperor his father published an edict, commanding all his subjects, upon great penalties, to break the smaller end of their eggs. The people so highly resented this law that our histories tell us there have been six rebellions raised on that account; wherein one Emperor lost his life,[1] and another his crown.[2] These civil commotions were constantly fomented by the monarchs of Blefuscu; and when they were quelled, the exiles always fled for refuge to that empire. It is computed that eleven thousand persons have, at several times, suffered death, rather than submit to break their eggs at the smaller end. Many hundred large volumes have been published upon this controversy. But the books of the Big Endians have been long forbidden, and the whole party rendered incapable.

"Now, the Big Endian exiles have found so much credit in the Emperor of Blefuscu's court, and so much private assistance and encouragement from their party here at home, that a bloody war has been carried on between the two empires for six and

[1] Charles I of England.
[2] James II of England.

thirty moons with various success. During this time
we have lost forty capital ships, and a much greater
number of smaller vessels, together with thirty thousand of our best seamen and soldiers; and the damage received by the enemy is reckoned to be somewhat greater than ours. However, they have now
equipped a numerous fleet, and are just preparing
to make a descent upon us. His Imperial Majesty,
placing great confidence in your valor and strength,
has commanded me to lay this account of his affairs
before you."

I desired the Secretary to present my humble duty
to the Emperor, and to let him know that I thought
it would not become me, who was a foreigner, to in-
terfere with parties; but I was ready, with the haz-
ard of my life, to defend his person and state against
all invaders.

CHAPTER 5

Gulliver Prevents an Invasion of Lilliput

THE EMPIRE OF BLEFUSCU is an island situated on the north-northeast side of Lilliput, from whence it is parted only by a channel of eight hundred yards wide. I had not yet seen it. And upon this notice of an intended invasion I avoided appearing on that side of the coast for fear of being discovered by some of the enemy's ships, who had received no intelligence of me, all intercourse between the two empires having been strictly forbidden during the war, upon pain of death, and an embargo laid by our Emperor upon all vessels whatsoever. I communicated to his Majesty a project I had formed of seizing the enemy's whole fleet, which, as our scouts assured us, lay at anchor in the harbor ready to sail with the first fair wind.

I consulted the most experienced seamen upon

the depth of the channel, which they had often plumbed. They told me that in the middle at high water it was seventy *glumgluffs* deep, which is about six feet of European measure; and the rest of it fifty *glumgluffs* at most. I walked toward the northeast coast over against Blefuscu; and lying down behind a hillock, took out my small pocket perspective glass and viewed the enemy's fleet at anchor, consisting of about fifty men-of-war and a great number of transports. I then came back to my house, and gave order (for which I had a warrant) for a great quantity of the strongest cable and bars of iron.

I was to hold my right foot in my left hand

[SEE PAGE 41]

The cable was about as thick as packthread, and the bars of the length and size of a knitting needle. I trebled the cable to make it stronger, and for the same reason I twisted three of the iron bars together, binding the extremities into a hook. Having thus fixed fifty hooks to as many cables, I went back to the northeast coast, and putting off my coat, shoes, and stockings, walked into the sea in my leather jerkin, about half an hour before high water. I waded with what haste I could, and swam in the middle about thirty yards till I felt ground. I arrived at the fleet in less than half an hour.

The enemy was so frighted when they saw me that they leaped out of their ships, and swam to shore, where there could not be fewer than thirty thousand souls. I then took my tackling, and fastening a hook to a hole at the prow of each, I tied all the cords together at the end. While I was thus employed, the enemy discharged several thousand arrows, many of which stuck in my hands and face; and besides the excessive smart, gave me much disturbance in my work. My greatest apprehension was for my eyes, which I should certainly have lost if I had not suddenly thought of an expedient. I kept among other little necessaries a pair of spectacles in a private pocket, which, as I observed before, had escaped the Emperor's searchers. These I took out and fastened as strongly as I could upon my nose, and thus armed went on boldly with my work in

spite of the enemy's arrows, many of which struck against the glasses of my spectacles, but without any other effect, further than a little to discompose them.

I now fastened all the hooks, and taking the knot in my hand, began to pull. But not a ship would stir, for they were all too fast held by their anchors, so that the boldest part of my enterprise remained. I therefore let go the cord, and leaving the hooks fixed to the ships, I resolutely cut with my knife the cables that fastened the anchors, receiving above two hundred shots in my face and hands. Then I took up the knotted end of the cables to which my hooks were tied, and with great ease drew fifty of the enemy's largest men-of-war after me.

The Blefuscudians, who had not the least imagination of what I intended, were at first confounded with astonishment. They had seen me cut the cables, and thought my design was only to let the ships run adrift or fall foul on each other, but when they perceived the whole fleet moving in order, and saw me pulling at the end, they set up such a scream of grief and despair that it is almost impossible to describe or conceive. When I had got out of danger, I stopped awhile to pick out the arrows that stuck in my hands and face, and rubbed on some of the same ointment that was given me at my first arrival. I then took off my spectacles, and waiting about an hour, till the tide was a little fallen, I waded through the middle with my cargo, and arrived safe at the royal port of Lilliput.

The Emperor and his whole court stood on the shore awaiting the issue of this great adventure. They saw the ships move forward in a large half moon, but could not discern me, who was up to my breast in water. When I advanced to the middle of the channel, they were yet in more pain, because I was underwater to my neck. The Emperor concluded me to be drowned, and that the enemy's fleet was approaching in a hostile manner. But he was soon eased of his fears, for the channel growing shallower every step I made, I came in a short time within hearing, and holding up the end of the cable by which the fleet was fastened, I cried in a loud voice, "Long live the most puissant Emperor of Lilli-put!" This great prince received me at my landing with all possible encomiums, and created me a *nardac* upon the spot, which is the highest title of honor among them.

His Majesty desired I would take some other opportunity of bringing all the rest of his enemy's ships into his ports. And so unmeasurable is the ambition of princes that he seemed to think of nothing less than reducing the whole empire of Blefuscu into a province, and governing it by a viceroy; of destroying the Big Endian exiles, and compelling that people to break the smaller end of their eggs, by which he would remain the sole monarch of the whole world. But I endeavored to divert him from this design by many arguments drawn from the topics of policy as well as justice; and I plainly protested that I would never be an instrument of bringing a free and brave people into slavery. And when the matter was debated in council, the wisest part of the ministry were of my opinion.

About three weeks after this exploit there arrived a solemn embassy from Blefuscu with humble offers of a peace, which was soon concluded upon conditions very advantageous to our Emperor. There were six ambassadors with a train of about five hundred persons, and their entry was very magnificent, suitable to the grandeur of their master and the im-

portance of their business. When their treaty was
finished, wherein I did them several good offices by
the credit I now had, or at least appeared to have at
court, their Excellencies, who were privately told
how much I had been their friend, made me a visit
in form. They began with many compliments upon
my valor and generosity, invited me to that kingdom
in their Emperor's name, and desired me to show
them some proofs of my prodigious strength, of
which they had heard so many wonders.

When I had for some time entertained their Excellencies, to their infinite satisfaction and surprise, I
desired they would do me the honor to present my
most humble respects to the Emperor their master,
the renown of whose virtues had so justly filled the
whole world with admiration, and whose royal person I resolved to attend before I returned to my own
country. Accordingly, the next time I had the honor
to see our Emperor, I desired his general license to
wait on the Blefuscudian monarch, which he was
pleased to grant me, as I could plainly perceive, in a
very cold manner. But I could not guess the reason,
till I had a whisper from a certain person, that Flimnap and Bolgolam had represented my intercourse
with those ambassadors as a mark of disaffection,
from which I am sure my heart was wholly free. And
this was the first time I began to conceive some imperfect idea of courts and ministers.

It is to be observed that these ambassadors spoke to me by an interpreter, the languages of both empires differing as much from each other as any two in Europe, and each nation priding itself upon the antiquity, beauty, and energy of their own tongues, with an avowed contempt for that of their neighbor. Yet our Emperor, standing upon the advantage he had got by the seizure of their fleet, obliged them to deliver their credentials and make their speech in the Lilliputian tongue. And it must be confessed that from the great intercourse of trade and commerce between both realms, and from the custom in each empire to send their young nobility and richer gentry to the other, there are few persons of distinction, or merchants, or seamen but what can hold conversation in both tongues. This I discovered some weeks after, when I went to pay my respects to the Emperor of Blefuscu, which, through the malice of my enemies, proved a very happy adventure to me.

CHAPTER 6

Lilliput's Laws, Customs,
and Educational Methods

LTHOUGH I INTEND to leave the description of this empire to a particular treatise, yet in the meantime I am content to gratify the curious reader with some general ideas. As the common size of the natives is somewhat under six inches high, so there is an exact proportion in all other animals, as well as plants and trees. For instance, the tallest horses and oxen are between four and five inches in height, the sheep an inch and a half, more or less: their geese about the bigness of a sparrow. And so the several gradations downward till you come to the smallest, which, to my sight, were almost invisible. But nature had adapted the eyes of the Lilliputians to all objects proper for their view. They see with great exactness, but at no great distance. And to show the sharpness of their sight toward objects that are

near, I have been much pleased with observing a
cook pulling a lark, which was not so large as a
common fly; and a young girl threading an invisible
needle with invisible silk. Their tallest trees are
about seven feet high; I mean some of those in
the great royal park, the tops whereof I could but
just reach with my fist clenched. The other vegetables are in the same proportion.

I shall say but little at present of their learning,
which for many ages had flourished in all its branches
among them. But their manner of writing is very
peculiar, being neither from the left to the right, like
the Europeans; nor from the right to the left, like the
Arabians; nor from up to down, like the Chinese; nor
from down to up, like the Cascagians; but aslant
from one corner of the paper to the other.

They bury their dead with their heads directly
downward, because they hold an opinion that in
eleven thousand moons they are all to rise again, in
which period the earth (which they conceive to be
flat) will turn upside down. By this means they shall,
at their resurrection, be found ready standing on
their feet. The learned among them confess the
absurdity of this doctrine, but the practice still
continues.

There are some laws and customs in this empire
very peculiar; and if they were not so directly contrary to those of my own dear country, I should be

tempted to say a little in their justification. It is only to be wished that they were as well executed. The first I shall mention relates to informers. All crimes against the state are punished here with the utmost severity; but if the person accused makes his innocence plainly to appear upon his trial, the accuser is immediately put to an ignominious death. And out of his goods or lands the innocent person is quad-

ruply recompensed for the loss of his time, for the
danger he underwent, for the hardship of his im-
prisonment, and for all the charges he had been at in
making his defense. Or, if that fund be deficient, it is
largely supplied by the Crown. The Emperor does
also confer on him some public mark of his favor, and
proclamation is made of his innocence through the
whole city.

They look upon fraud as a greater crime than
theft, and therefore seldom fail to punish it with
death. For they allege that care and vigilance, with
a very common understanding, may preserve a man's
goods from thieves, but honesty has no fence against
superior cunning. And since it is necessary that there
should be a perpetual intercourse of buying and
selling, and dealing upon credit, where fraud is permitted and connived at, or has no law to punish it,
the honest dealer is always undone, and the knave
gets the advantage.

Whoever can bring sufficient proof that he has
strictly observed the laws of his country for seventy-
three moons has a claim to certain privileges, according to his quality and condition of life, with a
proportionate sum of money out of a fund appropriated for that use.

In choosing persons for all employments they
have more regard to good morals than to great
abilities; for, since government is necessary to man-

kind, they believe that the common size of human understanding is fitted to some station or other, and that Providence never intended to make the management of public affairs a mystery, to be comprehended only by a few persons of sublime genius, of which there seldom are three born in an age. They suppose truth, justice, temperance, and the like, to be in every man's power; the practice of which virtues, assisted by experience and a good intention, would qualify any man for the service of his country, except where a course of study is required.

Ingratitude is among them a capital crime. They reason thus: whoever makes ill returns to his benefactor must needs be a common enemy to the rest of mankind, from whom he has received no obligation, and therefore such a man is not fit to live.

Their notions relating to the duties of parents and children differ extremely from ours. They will never allow, for instance, that a child is under any obligation to his father for begetting him, or his mother for bringing him into the world; which, considering the miseries of human life, was neither a benefit in itself nor intended so by his parents. Upon these and the like reasonings their opinion is that parents are the last of all others to be trusted with the education of their own children. And therefore they have in every town public nurseries, where all parents, except cottagers and laborers, are obliged to send

their infants of both sexes to be reared and educated
when they come to the age of twenty moons, at
which time they are supposed to have some rudiments of docility. These schools are of several kinds,
suited to different qualities and to both sexes. They
have certain professors well skilled in preparing
children for such a condition of life as befits the rank
of their parents, and their own capacities.

The nurseries for males of noble or eminent birth
are provided with grave and learned professors and
their several deputies. The clothes and food of the
children are plain and simple. They are bred up in
the principles of honor, justice, courage, modesty,
clemency, religion, and love of their country. They
are always employed in some business, except in the
times of eating and sleeping, which are very short,
and two hours for diversions, consisting of bodily
exercises. They are dressed by men till four years of
age, and then are obliged to dress themselves, although their quality be ever so great. And the
women attendants, who are aged proportionately
to ours at fifty, perform only the most menial offices.
They are never suffered to converse with servants,
but go together in small or greater numbers to take
their diversions. Their parents are suffered to see
them only twice a year; the visit is to last but an
hour. They are allowed to kiss the child at meeting
and parting; but a professor, who always stands by

on those occasions, will not suffer them to whisper, or use any fondling expressions, or bring any presents of toys, sweetmeats, and the like.

The nurseries for children of ordinary gentlemen, merchants, traders, and handicrafts are managed after the same manner. Those designed for trades are put out as apprentices at eleven years old, whereas those of persons of quality continue in their exercises till fifteen, which answers to one and twenty with us. But the confinement is gradually lessened for the last three years.

In the female nurseries the young girls of quality are educated much like the males, only they are dressed by orderly servants of their own sex; but always in the presence of a professor or deputy, till they come to dress themselves, which is at five years old. And if it be found that these nurses ever presume to entertain the girls with frightful or foolish stories, they are publicly whipped thrice about the city, imprisoned for a year, and banished for life to the most desolate part of the country. Thus the young ladies there are as much ashamed of being cowards and fools as the men, and despise all personal ornaments beyond decency and cleanliness.

Neither did I perceive any difference in their education, made by their difference of sex, only that the exercises of the females were not altogether so robust; and that some rules were given them relating to domestic life, and a smaller compass of learning was enjoined them. For their maxim is that among people of quality a wife should be always a reasonable and agreeable companion, because she cannot always be young. When the girls are twelve years old, which among them is the marriageable age, their parents or guardians take them home, with great expressions of gratitude to the professors, and seldom without tears of the young lady and her companions.

In the nurseries of females of the meaner sort the children are instructed in all kinds of work proper for their sex and their several degrees. Those intended for apprentices are dismissed at nine years old, the rest are kept to thirteen.

The poorer families who have children at these nurseries are obliged, besides their annual pension, which is as low as possible, to return to the steward of the nursery a small monthly share of their earnings, to be a portion for the child; and therefore all parents are limited in their expenses by the law. For the Lilliputians think nothing can be more unjust than for people, in subservience to their own appetites, to bring children into the world and leave the burden of supporting them on the public. As to persons of quality, they give security to appropriate a certain sum for each child, suitable to their condition; and these funds are always managed with good husbandry and the most exact justice.

The cottagers and laborers keep their children at home, their business being only to till and cultivate the earth, and therefore their education is of little consequence to the public. But the old and diseased among them are supported by hospitals, for begging is a trade unknown in this kingdom.

And here it may perhaps divert the curious reader to give some account of my domestics, and my manner of living in this country, during a residence of nine months and thirteen days. Having a head mechanically turned, and being likewise forced by necessity, I had made for myself a table and chair out of the largest trees in the royal park. Two hundred seamstresses were employed to make me shirts and linen for my bed and table, all of the strongest and coarsest kind they could get; which, however, they were forced to quilt together in several folds, for the thickest was some degrees finer than lawn. Their linen is usually three inches wide, and three feet make a piece.

The seamstresses took my measure as I lay on the ground, one standing at my neck, and another at my midleg, with a strong cord extended, that each held by the end, while the third measured the length of the cord with a rule an inch long. Then they measured my right thumb, and desired no more. For by a mathematical computation, that twice round the thumb is once round the wrist, and so on to the neck and the waist, and by the help of my old shirt, which I displayed on the ground before them for a pattern, they fitted me exactly.

Three hundred tailors were employed in the same manner to make me clothes. But they had another contrivance for taking my measure. I knelt down, and they raised a ladder from the ground to my neck. Upon this ladder one of them mounted, and let fall a plumb line from my collar to the floor, which just answered the length of my coat. But my waist and arms I measured myself. When my clothes were finished, which was done in my house (for the largest of theirs would not have been able to hold

them) they looked like the patchwork made by the
ladies in England, only that mine were all of a color.

I had three hundred cooks to dress my victuals in
little convenient huts built about my house, where
they and their families lived, and prepared me two
dishes apiece. I took up twenty waiters in my hand,
and placed them on the table. A hundred more attended below on the ground, some with dishes of
meat, and some with barrels of wine, and other
liquors, slung on their shoulders; all of which the
waiters above drew up as I wanted, in a very ingenious manner, by certain cords, as we draw the
bucket up a well in Europe. A dish of their meat was
a good mouthful and a barrel of their liquor a reasonable draught. Their mutton yields to ours, but
their beef is excellent. I have had a sirloin so large
that I have been forced to make three bites of it.
But this is rare. My servants were astonished to see
me eat it bones and all, as in our country we do the
leg of a lark. Their geese and turkeys I usually ate at
a mouthful, and I must confess they far exceed ours.
Of their smaller fowl I could take up twenty or thirty
at the end of my knife.

One day his Imperial Majesty, being informed of
my way of living, desired that himself and his Royal
Consort, with the young princes of the blood of
both sexes, might have the happiness of dining with
me. They came accordingly, and I placed them upon

chairs of state on my table, just over against me, with their guards about them. Flimnap, the Lord High Treasurer, attended there likewise with his white staff. And I observed he often looked on me with a sour countenance, which I would not seem to regard, but ate more than usual, in honor to my dear country as well as to fill the court with admiration. I have some private reasons to believe that this visit from his Majesty gave Flimnap an opportunity of doing me ill offices to his master. That minister had always been my secret enemy, though he outwardly caressed me more than was usual to the moroseness

of his nature. He represented to the Emperor the low condition of his treasury; that he was forced to take up money at great discount; that exchequer bills would not circulate under nine per cent below par; that in short I had cost his Majesty above a million and a half of *sprugs* (their greatest gold coin, about the bigness of a spangle); and upon the whole, that it would be advisable in the Emperor to take the first fair occasion of dismissing me.

The ladies and gentlemen of the court often came to call on me. On those occasions, it was my custom to go immediately to the door; and, after paying my respects, to take up the coach and two horses very carefully in my hands (for if there were six horses, the postillion always unharnessed four) and place them on a table, where I had fixed a movable rim quite round, of five inches high, to prevent accidents. And I have often had four coaches and horses at once on my table full of company, while I sat in my chair leaning my face toward them. And when I was engaged with one set, the coachmen would gently drive the others round my table. I have passed many an afternoon very agreeably in these conversations.

CHAPTER 7

Escape to Blefuscu

WHEN I WAS JUST PREPARING to pay my attendance on the Emperor of Blefuscu, a considerable person at court (to whom I had been very serviceable at a time when he lay under the highest displeasure of his Imperial Majesty) came to my house very privately at night in a close chair, and without sending his name, desired admittance. The chairmen were dismissed. I put the chair, with his Lordship in it, into my coat pocket, and giving orders to a trusty servant to say I was indisposed and gone to sleep, I fastened the door of my house, placed the chair on the table, according to my usual custom, and sat down by it. After the common salutations were over, observing his Lordship's countenance full of concern, and inquiring into the reason, he desired I would hear him with patience in a matter that highly concerned my honor and my life. His speech was to the following effect, for I took notes of it as soon as he left me.

"You are to know," said he, "that several committees of council have been lately called in the most private manner on your account; and it is but two days since his Majesty came to a full resolution.

"You are very sensible that Skyresh Bolgolam has been your mortal enemy almost ever since your arrival. His original reasons I know not, but his hatred is much increased since your great success against Blefuscu, by which his glory as admiral is obscured. This lord, in conjunction with Flimnap, the High Treasurer, and several others have prepared articles of impeachment against you for treason and other capital crimes."

This preface made me so impatient, being conscious of my own merits and innocence, that I was going to interrupt; but he entreated me to be silent, and thus proceeded.

"Out of gratitude for the favors you have done me, I procured information of the whole proceedings, and a copy of the articles, wherein I venture my head for your service."

Articles of Impeachment against Quinbus Flestrin
(the Man-Mountain)

ARTICLE I

That the said Quinbus Flestrin, having brought the Imperial fleet of Blefuscu into the royal port, and being afterward commanded by his Imperial Majesty to seize all the other ships of the said empire of Blefuscu, and reduce that empire to a province, to be governed by a viceroy from hence, and to destroy and put to death not only all the Big Endian exiles, but likewise all the people of that empire, who would not immediately forsake the Big Endian heresy: he, the said Flestrin, like a false traitor against his most Auspicious, Serene, Imperial Majesty, did petition to be excused from the said service upon pretense of unwillingness to force the consciences or destroy the liberties and lives of an innocent people.

ARTICLE II

That, whereas certain ambassadors arrived from the court of Blefuscu, to sue for peace in his Majesty's court: he, the said Flestrin, did, like a false traitor, aid, abet, comfort, and divert the said ambassadors, although he knew them to be servants to a prince who was lately an open enemy to his Imperial Majesty, and in open war against his said Majesty.

ARTICLE III

That the said Quinbus Flestrin, contrary to the duty of a faithful subject, is now preparing to make a voyage to the court and empire of Blefuscu, for which he had received only verbal license from his

Imperial Majesty; and under color of the said license, doth falsely and traitorously intend to take the said voyage, and thereby to aid, comfort, and abet the Emperor of Blefuscu, so late an enemy, and in open war with his Imperial Majesty aforesaid.

"There are some other articles, but these are the most important, of which I have read you an abstract.

"In the several debates upon this impeachment, it must be confessed that his Majesty gave many marks of his great lenity, often urging the services you had done him and endeavoring to extenuate your crimes. The Treasurer and Admiral insisted that you should be put to the most painful and ignominious death, by setting fire on your house at night, and the General was to attend with twenty thousand men armed with poisoned arrows to shoot you on the face and hands. Some of your servants were to have private orders to strew a poisonous juice on your shirts, which would soon make you tear your own flesh, and die in the utmost torture. The General came into the same opinion, so that for a long time there was a majority against you.

"Upon this incident, Reldresal, Principal Secretary for Private Affairs, who always approved himself your true friend, was commanded by the Emperor to deliver his opinion, which he accordingly did; and

therein justified the good thoughts you have of him.
He allowed your crimes to be great, but that still
there was room for mercy, the most commendable
virtue in a prince, and for which his Majesty was so
justly celebrated. He said, the friendship between
you and him was so well known to the world that
perhaps the most honorable board might think him
partial. However, in obedience to the command he
had received, he would freely offer his sentiments.
That if his Majesty, in consideration of your services,
and pursuant to his own merciful disposition, would
please to spare your life, and only give order to put
out both your eyes, he humbly conceived that by
this expedient justice might in some measure be
satisfied, and all the world would applaud the lenity
of the Emperor, as well as the fair and generous
proceedings of those who have the honor to be his
counselors. That the loss of your eyes would be no
impediment to your bodily strength, by which you
might still be useful to his Majesty. That blindness
is an addition to courage, by concealing dangers
from us; that the fear you had for your eyes was the
greatest difficulty in bringing over the enemy's fleet,
and it would be sufficient for you to see by the eyes
of the ministers, since the greatest princes do no
more.

"This proposal was received with the utmost disapprobation by the whole board. Bolgolam, the Ad-

miral, could not preserve his temper, but rising up in fury, said he wondered how the Secretary dared presume to give his opinion for preserving the life of a traitor; that the services you had performed were, by all true reasons of state, the great aggravation of your crimes; and the same strength which enabled you to bring over the enemy's fleet might serve, upon the first discontent, to carry it back; that he had good reasons to think you were a Big Endian in your heart; and as treason begins in the heart, before it appears in overt acts, so he accused you as a traitor on that account, and therefore insisted you should be put to death.

"The Treasurer was of the same opinion. He showed to what straits his Majesty's revenue was reduced by the charge of maintaining you, which would soon grow insupportable; that the Secretary's expedient of putting out your eyes was so far from being a remedy against this evil, it would probably increase it, as it is manifest from the common practice of blinding some kind of fowl, after which they fed the faster, and grew sooner fat; that his sacred Majesty and the Council, who are your judges, were in their own consciences fully convinced of your guilt, which was a sufficient argument to condemn you to death, without the formal proofs required by the strict letter of the law.

"But his Imperial Majesty, fully determined against capital punishment, was graciously pleased to say that since the Council thought the loss of your eyes too easy a censure, some other may be inflicted hereafter. And your friend the Secretary, humbly desiring to be heard again in answer to what the Treasurer had objected concerning the great charge his Majesty was at in maintaining you, said that his Excellency, who had the sole disposal of the Emperor's revenue, might easily provide against that evil by gradually lessening your establishment; by which, for want of sufficient food, you would grow weak and faint, and lose your appetite, and consequently decay and consume in a few months. Thus by the great friendship of the Secretary, the whole affair was compromised.

"In three days your friend the Secretary will be directed to come to your house, and read before you the articles of impeachment; and then to signify the great lenity and favor of his Majesty and Council, whereby you are only condemned to the loss of your eyes, which his Majesty does not question you will gratefully and humbly submit to. And twenty of his Majesty's surgeons will attend, in order to see the operation well performed, by discharging very sharp-pointed arrows into the balls of your eyes, as you lie on the ground.

"I leave to your prudence what measures you will take; and to avoid suspicion, I must immediately return in as private a manner as I came."

His Lordship did so, and I remained alone, under

many doubts and perplexities of mind. I must confess that, having never been designed for a courtier
either by my birth or education, I was so ill a judge
of things that I could not discover the lenity and
favor of the sentence, but conceived it rather to be
rigorous than gentle. I sometimes thought of standing my trial, for although I could not deny the facts
alleged in the several articles, yet I hoped they
would admit of some extenuations.

At last I fixed upon a resolution, and to it I owe
the preserving of my eyes, and consequently my
liberty. Having his Imperial Majesty's license to pay
my attendance upon the Emperor of Blefuscu, I took
this opportunity, before the three days were elapsed,
to send a letter to my friend the Secretary, signifying
my resolution of setting out that morning for Blefuscu, and without waiting for an answer, I went to
that side of the island where our fleet lay. I seized a
large man-of-war, tied a cable to the prow, and, lifting up the anchors, I stripped myself, put my clothes
(together with my coverlet, which I carried under
my arm) into the vessel, and drawing it after me between wading and swimming, arrived at the royal
port of Blefuscu, where the people had long expected me. They lent me two guides to direct me to
the capital city, which is of the same name. I held
them in my hands till I came within two hundred
yards of the gate, and desired them to signify my

arrival to one of the secretaries, and let him know I there waited his Majesty's commands.

I had an answer in about an hour, that his Majesty, attended by the Royal Family and great officers of the court, was coming out to receive me. I advanced a hundred yards. The Emperor and his train alighted from their horses, the Empress and ladies from their coaches, and I did not perceive they were in any fright or concern. I lay on the ground to kiss his Majesty's and the Empress's hand. I told his Majesty that I had come according to my promise, and with the license of the Emperor, my master, to have the honor of seeing so mighty a monarch, and to offer him any service in my power, consistent with my duty to my own prince. I did not mention a word about my disgrace.

I shall not trouble the reader with the particular account of my reception at this court, which was suitable to the generosity of so great a prince; [1] nor of the difficulties I was in for want of a house and bed, being forced to lie on the ground, wrapped up in my coverlet.

[1] Louis XIV.

CHAPTER 8

Gulliver Returns to His Native Country

THREE DAYS AFTER MY ARRIVAL, walking out of curiosity to the northeast coast of the island, I observed, about half a league off, in the sea, something that looked like a boat overturned. I pulled off my shoes and stockings, and wading two or three hundred yards, I found the object to approach nearer by force of the tide. And then I plainly saw it to be a real boat, which I supposed might, by some tempest, have been driven from a ship. Whereupon I returned immediately toward the city, and desired his Imperial Majesty to lend me twenty of the tallest vessels he had left after the loss of his fleet, and three thousand seamen under the command of his Vice-Admiral. This fleet sailed round, while I went back the shortest way to the coast where I first discovered the boat. I found the tide had driven it still nearer.

The seamen were all provided with cordage, which I had beforehand twisted to a sufficient strength. When the ships came up, I stripped myself, and waded till I came within a hundred yards of the boat, after which I was forced to swim till I got up to it. The seamen threw me the end of the cord, which I fastened to a hole in the forepart of the boat, and the other end to a man-of-war. But I found all my labor to little purpose; for being out of my depth, I was not able to work. In this necessity, I was forced to swim behind, and push the boat forward as often as I could, with one of my hands. And the tide favoring me, I advanced so far that I could just hold up my chin and feel the ground. I rested two or three minutes, and then gave the boat another shove, and so on till the sea was no higher than my armpits. Now, the most laborious part being over, I took out my other cables, which were stowed in one of the ships, and fastened them first to the boat and then to nine of the vessels which attended me. The wind being favorable, the seamen towed and I shoved till we arrived within forty yards of the shore. Then waiting till the tide was out, I got dry to the boat, and by the assistance of two thousand men, with ropes and engines, I made a shift to turn it on its bottom, and found it was but little damaged.

After great difficulties, I was by the help of certain paddles, which cost me ten days' making, able to get

my boat to the royal port of Blefuscu, where a
mighty concourse of people appeared upon my arrival, full of wonder at the sight of so prodigious a
vessel. I told the Emperor that my good fortune had
thrown this boat in my way to carry me to some
place from whence I might return into my native
country, and begged his Majesty's orders for getting
materials to fit it up, together with his license to depart; which, after some kind expostulations, he was
pleased to grant.

I did very much wonder, in all this time, not to
have heard of any express relating to me from our
Emperor to the court of Blefuscu. But I was afterward given privately to understand that his Imperial
Majesty, never imagining I had the least notice of
his designs, believed I was only gone to Blefuscu in
performance of my promise, according to the license
he had given me, which was well known at our court,
and would return in a few days when that ceremony
was ended. But he was at last in pain at my long absence. And after consulting with the Treasurer and
the rest of that cabal, a person of quality was dispatched with the copy of the articles against me.
This envoy had instructions to represent to the monarch of Blefuscu the great lenity of his master, who
was content to punish me no further than with the
loss of my eyes; that I had fled from justice, and if I
did not return in two hours, I should be deprived of

I lay down on my face to kiss his hand

my title of *nardac,* and declared a traitor. The envoy further added that, in order to maintain the peace and amity between both empires, his master expected that his brother of Blefuscu would give orders to have me sent back to Lilliput, bound hand and foot, to be punished as a traitor.

The Emperor of Blefuscu, having taken three days to consult, returned an answer consisting of many civilities and excuses. He said that, as for sending me bound, his brother knew it was impossible; that although I had deprived him of his fleet, yet he owed great obligations to me for many good offices I had done him in making the peace. That, however, both their Majesties would soon be made easy; for I had found a prodigious vessel on the shore, able to carry me on the sea, which he had given order to fit up with my own assistance and direction; and he hoped in a few weeks both empires would be freed from so insupportable an encumbrance.

With this answer the envoy returned to Lilliput, and the monarch of Blefuscu related to me all that had passed, offering me at the same time (but under the strictest confidence) his gracious protection, if I would continue in his service. Although I believed him sincere, yet I resolved never more to put any confidence in princes or ministers, where I could possibly avoid it. And therefore, with all due acknowledgments for his favorable intentions, I hum-

bly begged to be excused. I told him that since fortune, whether good or evil, had thrown a vessel in
my way, I was resolved to venture myself in the
ocean, rather than be an occasion of difference between two such mighty monarchs. Neither did I find
the Emperor at all displeased; and I discovered by a
certain accident that he was very glad of my resolution, and so were most of his ministers.

These considerations moved me to hasten my departure; to which the court, impatient to have me
gone, very readily contributed. Five hundred workmen were employed to make two sails to my boat,
according to my directions, by quilting thirteen folds
of their strongest linen together. I was at the pains
of making ropes and cables, by twisting ten, twenty
or thirty of the thickest and strongest of theirs. A
great stone that I happened to find, after a long
search, by the seashore, served me for an anchor. I
had the tallow of three hundred cows for greasing
my boat, and other uses. I was at incredible pains in
cutting down some of the largest timber trees for
oars and masts, wherein I was, however, much assisted by his Majesty's ship carpenters, who helped
me in smoothing them, after I had done the rough
work.

In about a month, when all was prepared, I sent
to receive his Majesty's commands, and to take my
leave. The Emperor and Royal Family came out of

the palace. I lay down on my face to kiss his hand, which he very graciously gave me. So did the Empress and young princes of the blood. His Majesty presented me with fifty purses of two hundred *sprugs* apiece, together with his picture at full length, which I put immediately into one of my gloves to keep it from being hurt. The ceremonies at my departure were too many to trouble the reader with at this time.

I stored the boat with the carcasses of a hundred oxen, and three hundred sheep, with bread and drink and as much meat ready dressed as four hundred cooks could provide. I took with me six cows and two bulls alive, with as many ewes and rams, intending to carry them into my own country and propagate the breed. And to feed them on board I had a good bundle of hay and a bag of corn. I would gladly have taken a dozen of the natives, but this was a thing the Emperor would by no means permit. And besides a diligent search into my pockets, his Majesty engaged my honor not to carry away any of his subjects, although with their own consent and desire.

Having thus prepared all things as well as I was able, I set sail on the 24th day of September, 1701, at six in the morning. And when I had gone about four leagues to the northward, the wind being at southeast, at six in the evening I descried a small island about half a league to the northwest. I advanced forward, and cast anchor on the lee side of the island, which seemed to be uninhabited. I then took some refreshment, and went to my rest. I slept well, and I conjecture at least six hours, for I found the day broke in two hours after I awaked. It was a clear night. I ate my breakfast before the sun was up. And heaving anchor, the wind being favorable, I steered the same course that I had done the day before, wherein I was directed by my pocket compass.

My intention was to reach, if possible, one of those islands which I had reason to believe lay to the northeast of Van Diemen's Land. I discovered nothing all that day. But upon the next, about three in the afternoon, when I had by my computation made twenty-four leagues from Blefuscu, I descried a sail steering to the southeast. My course was due east. I hailed her, but could get no answer; yet I found I gained upon her, for the wind slackened. I made all the sail I could, and in half an hour she spied me, then hung out her ancient, and discharged a gun.

It is not easy to express the joy I was in upon the unexpected hope of once more seeing my beloved country, and the dear pledges I had left in it. The ship slackened her sails, and I came up with her between five and six in the evening, September 26. My heart leapt within me to see her English colors. I put my cows and sheep into my coat pockets, and got on board with all my little cargo of provisions.

The vessel was an English merchantman, returning from Japan by the North and South Seas; the captain, Mr. John Biddle of Deptford, a very civil man, and an excellent sailor. There were about fifty men in the ship; and here I met an old comrade of mine, one Peter Williams, who gave me a good character to the captain. This gentleman treated me with kindness, and desired I would let him know what

place I came from last, and whither I was bound. I
answered in a few words, but he thought I was raving, and that the dangers I underwent had disturbed
my head; whereupon I took my black cattle and
sheep out of my pocket, which, after great astonishment, clearly convinced him of my veracity. I then
showed him the gold given me by the Emperor of
Blefuscu, together with his Majesty's picture at full
length, and some other rarities of that country. I
gave him two purses of two hundred *sprugs* each,
and promised, when we arrived in England, to make
him a present of a cow and a sheep.

We arrived in the Downs on the 13th of April,
1702. I had only one misfortune: the rats on board
carried away one of my sheep. I found her bones in
a hole, picked clean from the flesh. The rest of my
cattle I got safe on shore, and set them grazing in
a bowling green at Greenwich, where the fineness of
the grass made them feed very heartily, though I
had always feared the contrary. Neither could I possibly have preserved them in so long a voyage if the
captain had not allowed me some of his best biscuit,
which, rubbed to powder and mingled with water,
was their constant food.

The short time I continued in England I made
considerable profit by showing my cattle to many
persons of quality, and others. And before I began
my second voyage, I sold them for six hundred

pounds. Since my last return, I find the breed is considerably increased, especially the sheep; which I hope will prove much to the advantage of the woolen manufacture, by the fineness of the fleeces.

I stayed but two months with my wife and family; for my insatiable desire of seeing foreign countries would suffer me to continue no longer. I left fifteen hundred pounds with my wife, and fixed her in a good house at Redriff. My remaining stock I carried with me, part in money and part in goods, in hopes to improve my fortunes. My eldest uncle John had left me an estate in land, near Epping, of about thirty pounds a year; and I had a long lease of the Black Bull in Fetter Lane, which yielded me as much more; so that I was not in any danger of leaving my family upon the parish. My son Johnny, named so after his uncle, was at the Grammar School, and a towardly child. My daughter Betty (who is now well married, and has children) was then at her needlework. I took leave of my wife, and boy and girl, with tears on both sides, and went on board the *Adventure,* a merchant ship of three hundred tons, bound for Surat, India, Captain John Nicholas of Liverpool, commander.

Gulliver's Travels

PART II

A Voyage to Brobdingnag

CHAPTER 9

Gulliver Is Captured
by a Native

E SET SAIL in the *Adventure* on June 20, 1702, and had a good voyage till we arrived at the Cape of Good Hope. We landed for fresh water, but discovering a leak, we unshipped our goods and wintered there. Toward the end of March we sailed again. North of the island of Madagascar we ran into a terrible storm which lasted for twenty days and carried us far off our course.

After two days of perfect calm, the southern monsoon began to set in. It was a very fierce storm; the sea broke strange and dangerous. When it was over we brought the ship to. Our course was east-northeast, the wind was at southwest.

During this storm, we had been carried by my computation about five hundred leagues to the east, so that the oldest sailor on board could not tell in what part of the world we were. Our provisions held out well, our ship was stanch, and our crew all in good health; but we lay in the utmost distress for water.

On the 16th day of June, 1703, a boy on the top-mast discovered land. On the 17th we came in full view of a great island or continent (for we knew not which) on the south side whereof was a small neck of land jutting out into the sea, and a creek too shallow to hold a ship of above one hundred tons. We cast anchor within a league of this creek, and our captain sent a dozen of his men well armed in the longboat with vessels for water if any could be found. I desired his leave to go with them, that I might see the country and make what discoveries I could.

When we came to land we saw no river or spring, nor any sign of inhabitants. Our men therefore wandered on the shore to find out some fresh water near the sea, and I walked alone about a mile on the other side, where I observed the country all barren and rocky. I now began to be weary, and seeing nothing to entertain my curiosity, I returned gently down toward the creek; and the sea being full in my view, I saw our men already got into the boat, and rowing for life to the ship. I was going to halloo after them, although it had been to little purpose, when I observed a huge creature walking after them in the sea, as fast as he could. He waded not much deeper than his knees, and took prodigious strides, but our men had the start of him half a league, and the sea thereabouts being full of sharp-pointed rocks, the monster was not able to overtake the boat.

I did not stay to see the issue of that adventure, but ran as fast as I could the way I first went, and then climbed up a steep hill, which gave me some prospect of the country. I found it fully cultivated; but that which first surprised me was the length of the grass, which in those grounds that seemed to be kept for hay was about twenty feet high.

I came upon a highroad, for so I took it to be, though it served to the inhabitants only as a footpath through a field of barley. Here I walked on for some time, but could see little on either side, it being now near harvest and the corn rising at least forty feet. I was an hour walking to the end of this field, which was fenced in with a hedge of at least one hundred and twenty feet high, and the trees so lofty that I could make no computation of their altitude. There was a stile to pass from this field into the next. It had four steps, and a stone to cross over when you came to the uppermost. It was impossible for me to climb this stile, because every step was six feet high, and the upper stone above twenty.

I was endeavoring to find some gap in the hedge when I discovered one of the inhabitants in the next

field, advancing toward the stile, of the same size as
the one I saw in the sea pursuing our boat. He appeared as tall as an ordinary spire steeple, and took
about ten yards at every stride, as near as I could
guess. I was struck with the utmost fear and astonishment, and ran to hide myself in the corn, from
whence I saw him at the top of the stile, looking back
into the next field on the right hand, and heard him
call in a voice many degrees louder than a speaking
trumpet. But the noise was so high in the air that at
first I certainly thought it was thunder. Whereupon
seven monsters like himself came toward him with

reaping hooks in their hands, each hook about the size of six scythes.

These people were not so well clad as the first, whose servants or laborers they seemed to be. For upon some words he spoke, they went to reap the corn in the field where I lay. I kept at as great a distance from them as I could, but was forced to move with extreme difficulty, for the stalks of the corn were sometimes not above a foot distant, so that I could hardly squeeze my body between them. However, I made a shift to go forward till I came to a part of the field where the corn had been laid by the rain and wind. Here it was impossible for me to advance a step; for the stalks were so interwoven that I could not creep through, and the beards of the fallen ears so strong and pointed that they pierced through my clothes into my flesh. At the same time I heard the reapers not above a hundred yards behind me.

Being quite dispirited with toil and wholly overcome by grief and despair, I lay down between two ridges and heartily wished I might there end my days. I bemoaned my desolate widow and fatherless children. I lamented my own folly and willfulness in attempting a second voyage against the advice of all my friends and relations. In this terrible agitation of mind I could not forbear thinking of Lilliput, whose inhabitants looked upon me as the greatest prodigy that ever appeared in the world; where I was able to draw an imperial fleet in my hand and perform those other actions which will be recorded forever in the chronicles of that empire, while posterity shall hardly believe them, although attested by millions. I reflected what a mortification it must prove to me to appear as inconsiderable in this nation as one single Lilliputian would be among us.

But this I conceived was to be the least of my misfortunes. For as human creatures are observed to be more savage and cruel in proportion to their bulk, what could I expect but to be a morsel in the mouth of the first among these enormous barbarians that should happen to seize me?

One of the reapers approached within ten yards of the ridge where I lay, and I feared that with the next step I should be squashed to death under his foot or cut in two with his reaping hook. And therefore when he was again about to move, I screamed as loud as fear could make me. Whereupon the huge creature trod short, and looking round about under him for some time, at last espied me as I lay on the ground. He considered awhile with the caution of one who endeavors to lay hold on a small dangerous animal in such a manner that it shall not be able either to scratch or to bite him, as I myself have sometimes done with a weasel in England.

At length he ventured to take me up behind by the middle between his forefinger and thumb, and brought me within three yards of his eyes, that he might behold my shape more perfectly. I guessed his meaning, and my good fortune gave me so much presence of mind that I resolved not to struggle in the least as he held me in the air about sixty feet from the ground, although he grievously pinched my sides, for fear I should slip through his fingers. All I ventured was to raise my eyes toward the sun, and place my hands together in a supplicating posture,

and to speak some words in a humble melancholy tone, suitable to the condition I then was in. I feared every moment that he would dash me against the ground, as we usually do any little hateful animal which we have a mind to destroy.

But my good star would have it that he appeared pleased with my voice and gestures, and began to look upon me as a curiosity, much wondering to hear me pronounce articulate words, although he could not understand them. In the meantime I was not able to forbear groaning and shedding tears, and turning my head toward my sides, letting him know, as well as I could, how cruelly I was hurt by the pressure of his thumb and finger. He seemed to get my meaning; for, lifting up the lappet of his coat, he put me gently into it, and immediately ran along with me to his master, who was a substantial farmer and the same person I had first seen in the field.

The farmer, having received such an account of me as his servant could give him, took a piece of a small straw, about the size of a walking staff, and therewith lifted up the lappets of my coat; which it seems he thought to be some kind of covering that nature had given me. He blew my hair aside to take a better view of my face. He called his hinds about him and asked them, as I afterward learned, whether they had ever seen in the fields any little creature that resembled me. He then placed me softly on the ground upon all four, but I got immediately up, and walked slowly backward and forward, to let those people see I had no intent to run away.

They all sat down in a circle about me, the better to observe my motions. I pulled off my hat, and made

a low bow toward the farmer. I fell on my knees, and
lifted up my hands and eyes, and spoke several
words as loud as I could; I took a purse of gold out
of my pocket, and humbly presented it to him. He
received it on the palm of his hand, then applied it
close to his eye, to see what it was, and afterward
turned it several times with the point of a pin but
could make nothing of it. Whereupon I made a sign
that he should place his hand on the ground. I took
the purse, and opening it poured all the gold into his
palm. There were six Spanish pieces of four pistoles
each, besides twenty or thirty smaller coins. I saw
him wet the tip of his little finger upon his tongue
and take up one of my largest pieces, and then another, but he seemed to be wholly ignorant what
they were. He made me a sign to put them again into
my purse, and the purse again into my pocket,
which, after offering to him several times, I thought
it best to do.

The farmer by this time was convinced I must be
a rational creature. He spoke often to me, but the
sound of his voice pierced my ears like that of a
water mill, yet his words were articulate enough. I
answered as loud as I could, in several languages,
and he often laid his ear within two yards of me, but
all in vain, for we were wholly unintelligible to each
other. He then sent his servants to their work, and
taking his handkerchief out of his pocket, he dou-

bled and spread it on his left hand, which he placed flat on the ground, with the palm upward, making me a sign to step into it, as I could easily do, for it was not above a foot in thickness. I thought it my part to obey, and for fear of falling, laid myself at length upon the handkerchief, with the remainder of which he lapped me up to the head for further security, and in this manner carried me home to his house. There he called his wife, and showed me to her. But she screamed and ran back, as women in England do at the sight of a toad or a spider. However, when she had awhile seen my behavior, and how well I observed the signs her husband made, she was soon reconciled, and by degrees grew extremely tender of me.

It was about twelve at noon, and a servant brought in dinner. It was only one substantial dish of meat (fit for the plain condition of an husbandman) in a dish of about twenty-four feet in diameter. The company were the farmer and his wife, three children, and an old grandmother. When they sat down, the farmer placed me at some distance from him on the table, which was thirty feet high from the floor. I was in a terrible fright, and kept as far as I could from the edge for fear of falling.

The wife minced a bit of meat, then crumbled some bread on a trencher, and placed it before me. I made her a low bow, took out my knife and fork, and fell to eating, which gave them exceeding delight. The mistress sent her maid for a small dram cup, which held about three gallons, and filled it with drink. I took up the vessel with much difficulty in both hands, and in a most respectful manner drank to her Ladyship's health, expressing the words as loud as I could in English, which made the company laugh so heartily that I was almost deafened with the noise. This liquor tasted like a small cider, and was not unpleasant.

Then the master made me a sign to come to his trencher side; but as I walked on the table, I happened to stumble against a crust, and fell flat on my face, but received no hurt. I got up immediately, and observing the good people to be in much concern, I took my hat (which I held under my arm out of good manners) and waving it over my head, made three huzzas, to show I had got no mischief by my fall. But advancing forward toward my master (as I shall henceforth call him), his youngest son who sat next him, an arch boy of about ten years old, took me up by the legs, and held me so high in the air that I trembled in every limb. But his father snatched me from him, and at the same time gave him such a box on the left ear as would have felled an European troop of horse to the earth, ordering him to be taken from the table. But being afraid the boy might owe me a spite, and well remembering how mischievous all children among us naturally are to sparrows, rabbits, young kittens, and puppy dogs, I fell on my knees, and pointing to the boy, made my master to understand, as well as I could, that I desired his son might be pardoned. The father complied, and the lad took his seat again; whereupon I went to him and kissed his hand, which my master took, and made him stroke me gently with it.

In the midst of dinner, my mistress's favorite cat leaped into her lap. I heard a noise behind me like that of a dozen stocking weavers at work. Turning my head, I found it proceeded from the purring of this animal, who seemed to be three times larger than an ox, as I computed by the view of her head, and one of her paws, while her mistress was feeding and stroking her. The fierceness of this creature's countenance altogether discomposed me; though I stood at the farther end of the table, above fifty feet off, and although my mistress held her fast for fear she might give a spring and seize me in her talons. But it happened there was no danger; for the cat took not the least notice of me when my master placed me within three yards of her. And as I have been always told, and found true by experience in my travels, that flying or displaying fear before a fierce animal is a certain way to make it pursue or attack you, so I resolved in this dangerous juncture to show no manner of concern. I walked with intre-

pidity five or six times before the very head of the
cat, and came within half a yard of her; whereupon
she drew herself back, as if she were more afraid of

me. I had less apprehension concerning the dogs,
whereof three or four came into the room, as it is
usual in farmers' houses. One of them was a mastiff,
equal in bulk to four elephants, and a greyhound,
somewhat taller than the mastiff but not so large.

When dinner was almost done, the nurse came in
carrying a child of a year old who immediately spied
me and began a squall that you might have heard
from London Bridge to Chelsea, after the usual ora-
tory of infants, to get me for a plaything. The mother

out of pure indulgence took me up and put me toward the child, who presently seized me by the middle and got my head in his mouth, where I roared so loud that the urchin was frightened and let me drop; and I should certainly have broken my neck if the mother had not held her apron under me. The nurse to quiet her babe made use of a rattle, which was a kind of hollow vessel filled with great stones, and fastened by a cable to the child's waist: but all in vain, so that she was forced to apply the last remedy by giving it milk.

When dinner was done, my master went out to his laborers, and as I could discover by his voice and gesture, gave his wife a strict charge to take care of me. I was very much tired, and disposed to sleep, which my mistress perceiving, she put me on her own bed, and covered me with a clean white handkerchief, but larger and coarser than the mainsail of a man-of-war.

I slept about two hours, and dreamed I was at home with my wife and children, which aggravated my sorrows when I awakened and found myself alone in a vast room, between two and three hundred feet wide, and above two hundred high, lying in a bed twenty yards wide. My mistress was gone about her household affairs, and had locked me in. The bed was eight yards from the floor. Although desiring to get down, I dared not call; and it would have been in vain at so great a distance from the room where I lay to the kitchen where the family kept.

While I was under these circumstances, two rats crept up the curtains, and ran smelling backward and forward on the bed. One of them came up almost to my face, whereupon I rose in a fright, and drew out my sword to defend myself. These horrible animals had the boldness to attack me on both sides, and one of them held his forefeet at my collar. But I had the good fortune to rip up his belly before he could do me any mischief. He fell down at my feet, and the other, seeing the fate of his comrade, made

his escape, but not without one good wound on the back, which I gave him as he fled, and made the blood run trickling from him.

After this exploit, I walked gently to and fro on the bed, to recover my breath and loss of spirits. These creatures were of the size of a large mastiff, but infinitely more nimble and fierce, so that if I had taken off my belt before I went to sleep I must have been torn to pieces and devoured. I measured the tail of the dead rat, and found it to be two yards long, wanting an inch. But it went against my stomach to drag the carcass off the bed, where it lay still bleeding; I observed it had yet some life, but with a strong slash cross the neck, I dispatched it.

Soon after, my mistress came into the room, and seeing me all bloody, ran and took me up in her hand. I pointed to the dead rat, smiling and making other signs to show I was not hurt, whereat she was extremely rejoiced, calling the maid to take up the dead rat with a pair of tongs, and throw it out of the window. Then she set me on a table, where I showed her my sword all bloody; then wiping it on the lappet of my coat, I returned it to the scabbard.

CHAPTER 10

Gulliver Is Taken to the City

MY MISTRESS had a daughter of nine years old, a child mature for her age, very dexterous at her needle, and skillful in dressing her doll. Her mother and she contrived to fit up the doll's cradle for me against night. The cradle was put into a small drawer of a cabinet, and the drawer placed upon a hanging shelf for fear of the rats. This was my bed all the time I stayed with those people, though made more convenient by degrees, as I began to learn their language and make my wants known. This young girl was so handy that after I had once or twice pulled off my clothes before her, she was able to dress and undress me, though I never gave her that trouble when she would let me do either myself.

She made me seven shirts, and some other linen, of as fine cloth as could be got, which indeed was

coarser than sackcloth; and these she constantly
washed for me with her own hands. She was likewise
my schoolmistress to teach me the language. When
I pointed to anything, she told me the name of it in
her own tongue, so that in a few days I was able to
call for whatever I had a mind to. She was very good-
natured, and not above forty feet high, being little
for her age. She gave me the name of *Grildrig*, which
the family took up, and afterward the whole kingdom. The word imports what the Latins call *nanun-
culus*, the Italians *homunceletino*, and the English
mannikin. To her I chiefly owe my preservation in
that country: we never parted while I was there; I
called her my *glumdalclitch*, or little nurse: and I
should be guilty of great ingratitude if I omitted
this honorable mention of her care and affection toward me.

It now began to be known and talked of in the
neighborhood that my master had found a strange
animal in the field, about the bigness of a *splacknuck*, but exactly shaped in every part like a human
creature; which it likewise imitated in all its actions;
seemed to speak in a little language of its own, had
already learned several words of theirs, went erect
upon two legs, was tame and gentle, would come
when it was called, do whatever it was bid, had the
finest limbs in the world, and a complexion fairer
than a nobleman's daughter of three years old.

Another farmer who lived hard by, and was a particular friend of my master, came on a visit on purpose to inquire into the truth of this story. I was immediately produced, and placed upon a table, where I walked as I was commanded, drew my sword, put it up again, made my reverence to my master's guest, asked him in his own language how he did, and told him he was welcome, just as my little nurse had instructed me. This man, who was old and dimsighted, put on his spectacles to behold me better, at which I could not forbear laughing very heartily, for his eyes appeared like the full moon shining into a chamber at two windows. Our people, who discovered the cause of my mirth, bore me company in laughing, at which the old fellow was fool enough to be angry and out of countenance.

He had the character of a great miser, and to my misfortune he well deserved it, by the cursed advice he gave my master to show me as a sight upon a market day in the next town, which was half an hour's riding, about twenty-two miles from our house. I guessed there was some mischief contriving, when I observed my master and his friend whispering long together, sometimes pointing at me. And my fears made me fancy that I overheard and understood some of their words.

But the next morning Glumdalclitch, my little nurse, told me the whole matter, which she had cunningly picked out from her mother. The poor girl laid me on her bosom, and fell weeping with shame and grief. She apprehended some mischief would happen to me from rude vulgar folks, who might squeeze me to death or break one of my limbs by taking me in their hands. She had also observed how modest I was in my nature, how nicely I regarded my honor, and what an indignity I should conceive it to be exposed for money as a public spectacle to the meanest of the people. She said her papa and mamma had promised that Grildrig should be hers, but now she found they meant to serve her as they did last year, when they pretended to give her a lamb, and yet, as soon as it was fat, sold it to a butcher.

For my own part, I may truly affirm that I was less concerned than my nurse. I had a strong hope which never left me, that I should one day recover my liberty. And as to the ignominy of being carried about for a monster, I considered myself to be a perfect stranger in the country, and that such a misfortune could never be charged upon me as a reproach, if ever I should return to England; since the King of Great Britain himself, in my condition, must have undergone the same distress.

My master, pursuant to the advice of his friend, carried me in a box the next market day to the neighboring town, and took along with him his little daughter, my nurse, upon a pillion behind him. The box was close on every side, with a little door for me to go in and out, and a few gimlet holes to let in air. The girl had been so careful to put the quilt of her doll's bed into it, for me to lie down on. However, I was terribly shaken and discomposed in this journey, though it were but of half an hour. For the horse went about forty feet at every step, and trotted so high that the agitation was equal to the rising and falling of a ship in a great storm, but much more frequent.

Our journey was somewhat farther than from London to St. Albans. My master alighted at an inn which he used to frequent. And after consulting awhile with the innkeeper, and making some necessary preparations, he hired the *grultrud,* or crier, to give notice through the town of a strange creature to be seen at the Sign of the Green Eagle, not so big as a *splacknuck* (an animal in that country very finely shaped, about six feet long) and in every part of the body resembling a human creature, could speak several words, and perform a hundred diverting tricks.

I was placed upon a table in the largest room of the inn, which might be near three hundred feet square. My little nurse stood on a low stool close to the table, to take care of me and direct what I should do. My master, to avoid a crowd, would suffer only thirty people at a time to see me. I walked about on

the table as the girl commanded. She asked me questions as far as she knew my understanding of the language reached, and I answered them as loud as I
could. I turned about several times to the company,
paid my humble respects, said they were welcome,
and used some other speeches I had been taught. I
took up a thimble filled with liquor, which Glumdalclitch had given me for a cup, and drank their
health. I drew out my sword, and flourished it after
the manner of fencers in England. My nurse gave
me part of a straw, which I exercised as a pike, having learned the art in my youth.

I was that day shown to twelve sets of company,
and as often forced to go over again with the same
fopperies till I was half dead with weariness and vex-
ation. For those who had seen me made such wonderful reports that the people were ready to break
down the doors to come in. My master for his own interest would not suffer anyone to touch me except
my nurse. And, to prevent danger, benches were set
around the table at such a distance as put me out of
everybody's reach. However, an unlucky schoolboy
aimed a hazelnut directly at my head, which very
narrowly missed me. Otherwise, it came with so
much violence that it would have knocked out my
brains, for it was almost as large as a small pumpion.[1]
But I had the satisfaction to see the young rogue well
beaten, and turned out of the room.

[1] Pumpkin.

My master gave public notice that he would show me again the next market day, and in the meantime he prepared a more convenient vehicle for me, which he had reason enough to do, for I was so tired with my first journey and with entertaining company for eight hours together that I could hardly stand upon my legs or speak a word. It was at least three days before I recovered my strength. And that I might have no rest at home, all the neighboring gentlemen from a hundred miles around, hearing of my fame, came to see me at my master's own house. There could not be fewer than thirty persons with their wives and children (for the country is very populous); and my master demanded the rate of a full room whenever he showed me at home, although it were only to a single family. So that for some time I had but little ease every day of the week (except Wednesday, which is their Sabbath) although I was not carried to the town.

My master, finding how profitable I was likely to be, resolved to carry me to the most considerable cities of the kingdom. Having therefore provided himself with all things necessary for a long journey, and settled his affairs at home, he took leave of his wife, and upon the 17th of August, 1703, about two months after my arrival, we set out for the metropolis, situated near the middle of that empire, and about three thousand miles distance from our house. My master made his daughter Glumdalclitch ride

behind him. She carried me on her lap in a box tied
about her waist. The girl had lined it on all sides with
the softest cloth she could get, well quilted under-
neath, furnished it with her doll's bed, provided me
with linen and other necessaries, and made every-

thing as convenient as she could. We had no other
company but a boy of the house, who rode after us
with the luggage.

My master's design was to show me in all the
towns by the way, and to step out of the road for

*The Queen commanded her own cabinetmaker
to contrive a box for a bedchamber*

[SEE PAGE 129]

fifty or a hundred miles, to any village or person of quality's house where he might expect custom. We made easy journeys of not above seven or eight score miles a day. Glumdalclitch, on purpose to spare me, complained she was tired with the trotting of the horse. She often took me out of my box at my own desire, to give me air and show me the country, but always held me fast by a leading string. We passed over five or six rivers many degrees broader and deeper than the Nile or the Ganges; and there was hardly a rivulet so small as the Thames at London Bridge. We were ten weeks in our journey, and I was shown in eighteen large towns besides many villages and private families.

On the 26th day of October, we arrived at the metropolis, called in their language *Lorbrulgrud,* or Pride of the Universe. My master took a lodging in the principal street of the city, not far from the royal palace, and put out bills in the usual form, containing an exact description of my person and parts. He hired a large room between three and four hundred feet wide. He provided a table sixty feet in diameter, upon which I was to act my part, and palisadoed it around three feet from the edge, and as many high, to prevent my falling over. I was shown ten times a day, to the wonder and satisfaction of all people. I could now speak the language tolerably well, and perfectly understood every word that was spoken to me. Besides, I had learned their alphabet, and could make a shift to explain a sentence here and there; for Glumdalclitch had been my instructor while we were at home, and at leisure hours during our journey. She carried a little book in her pocket, not much larger than a Sanson's Atlas. It was a common treatise for the use of young girls, giving a short account of their religion. Out of this she taught me my letters, and interpreted the words.

CHAPTER 11

The Queen Buys Gulliver from the Farmer

THE FREQUENT LABORS I underwent every day made in a few weeks a very considerable change in my health. The more my master got by me, the more insatiable he grew. I had quite lost my appetite, and was almost reduced to a skeleton. The farmer observed it, and concluding I soon must die, resolved to make as good a hand of me as he could. While he was thus reasoning and resolving with himself, a *slardral*, or gentleman usher, came from court, commanding my master to carry me immediately thither for the diversion of the Queen and her ladies. Some of the latter had already been to see me, and reported strange things of my beauty, behavior, and good sense.

Her Majesty and those who attended her were beyond measure delighted with my demeanor. I fell on my knees, and begged the honor of kissing her

Imperial foot. But this gracious princess held out her little finger toward me (after I was set on a table), which I embraced in both my arms, and put the tip of it with the utmost respect to my lip. She made me some general questions about my country and my travels, which I answered as distinctly and in as few words as I could. She asked whether I would be content to live at court. I bowed down to the board of the table, and humbly answered that I was my master's slave, but if I were at my own disposal I should be proud to devote my life to her Majesty's service. She then asked my master whether he were willing to sell me at a good price. He, who apprehended I could not live a month, was ready enough to part with me, and demanded a thousand pieces of gold, which were ordered him on the spot, each piece being about the bigness of eight hundred moidores. But, allowing for the proportion of all things between that country and Europe, and the high price of gold among them, this was hardly so great a sum as a thousand guineas would be in England.

I then said to the Queen, since I was now her Majesty's most humble creature and vassal, I must beg the favor that Glumdalclitch, who had always tended me with so much care and kindness, and understood to do it so well, might be admitted into her service, and continue to be my nurse and instructor. Her Majesty agreed to my petition, and easily got the farmer's consent, who was glad enough to have his daughter preferred at court. The poor girl herself was not able to hide her joy. My late master withdrew, bidding me farewell, and saying he had left me in a good service; to which I replied not a word, only making him a slight bow.

The Queen observed my coldness, and when the farmer was gone out of the apartment, asked me the reason. I made bold to tell her Majesty that I owed no other obligation to my late master, than his not dashing out the brains of a poor harmless creature found by chance in his field; which obligation was amply recompensed by the gain he had made in showing me through half the kingdom, and the price he had now sold me for. That the life I had since led was laborious enough to kill an animal of ten times my strength. That my health was much impaired by the continual drudgery of entertaining the rabble every hour of the day, and that if my master had not thought my life in danger, her Majesty perhaps would not have got so cheap a bargain. But as I was out of all fear of being ill treated under the protection of so great and good an Empress, the Ornament of Nature, the Darling of the World, the Delight of her Subjects, the Phoenix of the Creation, so I hoped my late master's apprehensions would appear to be groundless, for I already found my spirits to revive by the influence of her most august presence.

This was the sum of my speech, delivered with great hesitation. The latter part was altogether framed in the style peculiar to that people, whereof I learned some phrases from Glumdalclitch, while she was carrying me to court.

The Queen, giving great allowance for my defectiveness in speaking, was, however, surprised at so much wit and good sense in so diminutive an animal. She took me in her own hand, and carried me to the King, who was then retired to his cabinet. His Majesty, a prince of much gravity and austere countenance, not well observing my shape at first view, asked the Queen after a cold manner how long it was since she grew fond of a *splacknuck;* for such it seems he took me to be as I lay upon my breast in her Majesty's right hand. But this princess, who has an infinite deal of wit and humor, set me gently on my feet upon the desk, and commanded me to give his Majesty an account of myself. This I did in a very few words, and Glumdalclitch, who attended at the cabinet door and could not endure I should be out of her sight, being admitted, confirmed all that had passed from my arrival at her father's house.

The King, although he be as learned a person as any in his dominions, and had been educated in the study of philosophy, and particularly mathematics, yet when he observed my shape exactly, and saw me walk erect, before I began to speak, conceived I

might be a piece of clockwork (which is in that country arrived to a very great perfection) contrived by
some ingenious artist. But when he heard my voice
and found what I delivered to be regular and rational he could not conceal his astonishment. He was
by no means satisfied with the relation I gave him of
the manner I came into his kingdom, but thought it
a story concerted between Glumdalclitch and her
father, who had taught me a set of words to make
me sell at a higher price. Upon this imagination he
put several other questions to me, and still received
rational answers, no otherwise defective than by a
foreign accent and an imperfect knowledge in the
language, with some rustic phrases which I had
learned at the farmer's house and did not suit the polite style of a court.

His Majesty sent for three great scholars who were
then in their weekly waiting, according to the custom in that country. These gentlemen, after they
had awhile examined my shape with much nicety,
were of different opinions concerning me. They all
agreed that I could not be produced according to the
regular laws of nature, because I was not framed
with a capacity of preserving my life, either by swiftness, or climbing of trees, or digging holes in the
earth.

They observed by my teeth, which they viewed
with great exactness, that I was a carnivorous ani-

mal; yet most quadrupeds being an overmatch for me, and field mice, with some others, too nimble, they could not imagine how I should be able to support myself, unless I fed upon snails and other insects, which they offered, by many learned arguments, to evince that I could not possibly do. They would not allow me to be a dwarf, because my littleness was beyond all degrees of comparison; for the Queen's favorite dwarf, the smallest ever known in that kingdom, was nearly thirty feet high. After much debate, they concluded unanimously that I was a freak of nature.

After this decisive conclusion, I entreated to be heard a word or two. I applied myself to the King, and assured his Majesty that I came from a country which abounded with several millions of both sexes, and of my own stature; where the animals, trees, and houses were all in proportion, and where by consequence I might be as able to defend myself, and to find sustenance, as any of his Majesty's subjects could do here; which I took for a full answer to those gentlemen's arguments. To this they only replied with a smile of contempt, saying that the farmer had instructed me very well in my lesson. The King, who had a much better understanding, dismissed his learned men and sent for the farmer, who by good fortune was not yet gone out of town. Having therefore first examined him privately, and then confronted him with me and the young girl, his Majesty began to think that what we told him might possibly be true. He desired the Queen to order that a particular care should be taken of me, and was of opinion that Glumdalclitch should still continue in her office of tending me, because he observed we had a great affection for each other. A convenient apartment was provided for her at court. She had a sort of governess appointed to take care of her education, a maid to dress her, and two other servants for menial offices; but the care of me was wholly appropriated to herself.

The Queen commanded her own cabinetmaker to contrive a box that might serve me for a bedchamber, after the model that Glumdalclitch and I should agree upon. This man was a most ingenious artist, and according to my directions, in three weeks finished for me a wooden chamber of sixteen feet square, and twelve high, with sash windows, a door, and two closets, like a London bedchamber. The board that made the ceiling was to be lifted up and down by two hinges, to put in a bed ready furnished by her Majesty's upholsterer, which Glumdalclitch took out every day to air, made it with her own hands, and letting it down at night, locked up the roof over me. A nice workman, who was famous for little curiosities, undertook to make me two chairs, with backs and frames, of a substance not unlike

ivory, and two tables, with a cabinet to put my
things in.

The room was quilted on all sides, as well as the
floor and the ceiling, to prevent any accident from
the carelessness of those who carried me, and to
break the force of a jolt when I went in a coach. I
desired a lock for my door, to prevent rats and mice
from coming in. The smith, after several attempts,
made the smallest that ever was seen among them,
for I have known a larger at the gate of a gentleman's
house in England. I made a shift to keep the key in
a pocket of my own, fearing Glumdalclitch might
lose it.

The Queen likewise ordered the thinnest silks that
could be got, to make me clothes, not much thicker
than an English blanket, very cumbersome till I was
accustomed to them. They were after the fashion of
the kingdom, partly resembling the Persian, and
partly the Chinese, and are a very grave and decent
habit.

The Queen became so fond of my company that
she could not dine without me. I had a table placed
upon the same at which her Majesty ate, just at her
left elbow, and a chair to sit on. Glumdalclitch stood
upon a stool on the floor, near my table, to assist and
take care of me. I had an entire set of silver dishes
and plates, and other necessaries, which, in proportion to those of the Queen, were not much bigger
than what I have seen of the same kind in a London

toy shop, for the furniture of a dollhouse. These my little nurse kept in her pocket in a silver box, and gave me at meals as I wanted them, always cleaning them herself.

No person dined with the Queen but the two Princesses Royal, the elder sixteen years old and the younger at that time thirteen and a month. Her Majesty used to put a bit of meat upon one of my dishes, out of which I carved for myself, and her diversion was to see me eat in miniature. For the Queen (who had indeed but a weak stomach) took up at one mouthful as much as a dozen English farmers could eat at a meal, which to me was for some time a very nauseous sight. She would crunch the wing of a lark, bones and all, between her teeth, although it were nine times as large as that of a full-grown turkey; and put a bit of bread into her mouth, as big as two twelvepenny loaves. She drank out of a golden cup, above a hogshead at a draught. Her knives were twice as long as a scythe set straight upon the handle. The spoons, forks, and other instruments were all in the same proportion. I remember when Glumdalclitch carried me out of curiosity to see some of the tables at court, where ten or a dozen of these enormous knives and forks were lifted up together, I thought I had never till then beheld so terrible a sight.

It is the custom that every Wednesday (which, as I have before observed, was their Sabbath) the King and Queen, with the royal issue of both sexes, dine together in the apartment of his Majesty, to whom I was now become a great favorite. And at these times my little chair and table were placed at his left hand, before one of the salt cellars. This prince took a pleasure in conversing with me, inquiring into the manners, religion, laws, government, and learning of Europe; wherein I gave him the best account I was

able. His apprehension was so clear and his judgment so exact that he made very wise reflections and observations upon all I said.

But, I confess that after I had been a little too copious in talking of my own beloved country, of our trade, and wars by sea and land, of our schisms in religion, and parties in the state, the prejudices of his education prevailed so far that he could not forbear taking me up in his right hand and stroking me gently with the other, after an hearty fit of laughing, asked me whether I were a Whig or a Tory. Then turning to his first minister, who waited behind him with a white staff, near as tall as the mainmast of the *Royal Sovereign,* he observed how contemptible a thing was human grandeur, which could be mimicked by such diminutive insects as I. "And yet," said he, "I dare engage, these creatures have their titles and distinctions of honor, they contrive little nests and burrows, that they call houses and cities; they make a figure in dress and equipage; they love, they fight, they dispute, they cheat, they betray." And thus he continued on, while my color came and went several times with indignation to hear our noble country— the mistress of arts and arms, the scourge of France, the arbitress of Europe, the seat of virtue, piety, honor and truth, the pride and envy of the world— so contemptuously treated.

But as I was not in a condition to resent injuries,

so, upon mature thoughts, I began to doubt whether I were injured or not. For, after having been accustomed several months to the sight and converse of this people, and observed every object upon which I cast my eyes to be of proportionate magnitude, the horror I had first conceived from their bulk and aspect was so far worn off that if I had then beheld a company of English lords and ladies in their finery and best day clothes, acting their several parts in the most courtly manner, of strutting, and bowing, and prating, to say the truth, I should have been strongly tempted to laugh as much at them as the King and his grandees did at me. Neither indeed could I forbear smiling at myself, when the Queen used to place me upon her hand toward a looking glass, by which both our persons appeared before me in full view together! And there could be nothing more ridiculous than the comparison; so that I really began to imagine myself dwindled many degrees below my usual size.

Nothing angered and mortified me so much as the Queen's dwarf, who being of the lowest stature that was ever in that country, became insolent at seeing a creature so much beneath him that he would always affect to swagger and look big as he passed by me in the Queen's antechamber, while I was standing on some table talking with the lords or ladies of the court. And he seldom failed of a smart word or

two upon my littleness; against which I could only revenge myself by calling him brother, challenging him to wrestle, and such repartees as are usual in the mouths of court pages.

One day at dinner this malicious little cub was so nettled with something I had said to him that raising himself upon the frame of her Majesty's chair he took me up by the middle, as I was sitting down, not thinking any harm, and let me drop into a large silver bowl of cream, and then ran away as fast as he could. I fell over head and ears, and if I had not been a good swimmer, it might have gone very hard with me. For Glumdalclitch in that instant happened to be at the other end of the room and the Queen was in such a fright that she wanted presence of mind to assist me. But my little nurse ran to my relief, and took me out, after I had swallowed above a quart of cream. I was put to bed, but I received no other damage than the loss of a suit of clothes, which was utterly spoiled. The dwarf was soundly whipped, and as a further punishment, forced to drink up the bowl of cream into which he had thrown me. Neither was he ever restored to favor. Soon after, the Queen bestowed him to a lady of high quality, so that I saw him no more, to my very great satisfaction, for I could not tell to what extremity such a malicious urchin might have carried his resentment.

He had before served me a scurvy trick, which set the Queen a-laughing, although at the same time she was heartily vexed and would have immediately cashiered him if I had not been so generous as to intercede. Her Majesty had taken a marrow bone upon her plate, and after knocking out the marrow, placed the bone again in the dish erect as it stood before. The dwarf, watching his opportunity, while Glumdaclitch was gone to the sideboard, mounted upon the stool she stood on to take care of me at meals, took me up in both hands, and squeezing my legs together, wedged them into the marrow bone above my waist, where I stuck for some time and made a very ridiculous figure. I believe it was near a minute before anyone knew what was become of me, for I thought it below me to cry out. But, as princes seldom get their meat hot, my legs were not scalded, only my stockings and breeches in a sad condition. The dwarf at my entreaty had no other punishment than a sound whipping.

I was frequently rallied by the Queen upon account of my fearfulness, and she used to ask me whether the people of my country were as great cowards as myself. The occasion was this. The kingdom is much pestered with flies in summer. And these odious insects, each of them as big as a Dunstable lark, hardly gave me any rest while I sat at dinner, with their continual humming and buzzing about my ears. They would sometimes alight upon my victuals and sometimes would fix upon my nose or forehead, where they stung me to the quick. I had

much ado to defend myself against these detestable
animals, and could not forbear starting when they
came on my face. It was the common practice of the
dwarf to catch a number of these insects in his hand,
as schoolboys do among us, and let them out suddenly under my nose, on purpose to frighten me, and
divert the Queen.

I remember one morning when Glumdalclitch
had set me in my box upon a window, as she usually
did in fair days, to give me air after I had lifted up
one of my sashes and sat down at my table to eat a
piece of sweet cake for my breakfast, above twenty
wasps, allured by the smell, came flying into the
room, humming louder than the drones of as many
bagpipes. Some of them seized my cake, and carried
it piecemeal away, others flew about my head and
face, confounding me with the noise and putting me
in the utmost terror of their stings. However, I had
the courage to rise and draw my sword, and attack
them in the air. I dispatched four of them, but the
rest got away, and I presently shut my window.

These insects were as large as partridges: I took
out their stings, found them an inch and a half long,
and as sharp as needles. I carefully preserved them
all, and having since shown them with some other
curiosities in several parts of Europe, upon my return to England I gave three of them to Gresham
College, and kept the fourth for myself.

CHAPTER 12

Gulliver Shows His
Skill in Navigation

I NOW INTEND to give the reader a short description of this country, as far as I traveled in it, which was not above two thousand miles round Lorbrulgrud, the metropolis. For the Queen, whom I always attended, never went farther when she accompanied the King in his progresses, and there stayed until his Majesty returned from viewing his frontiers. The whole extent of this prince's dominions reaches about six thousand miles in length, and from three to five in breadth. From this I cannot but conclude that our geographers of Europe are in a great error, by supposing nothing but sea between Japan and California. They ought to correct their maps and charts, by joining this vast tract of land to the northwest parts of America.

The kingdom is a peninsula, terminated to the northeast by a ridge of mountains thirty miles high,

which are altogether impassable by reason of the
volcanoes upon the tops. Neither do the most learned
know what sort of mortals inhabit beyond those
mountains, or whether they be inhabited at all. On
the three other sides it is bounded by the ocean.
There is not one seaport in the whole kingdom, and
those parts of the coasts into which the rivers issue
are so full of pointed rocks, and the sea generally so
rough, that there is no venturing with the smallest of
their boats, so that these people are wholly excluded
from any commerce with the rest of the world.

But the large rivers are full of vessels, and abound
with excellent fish, for they seldom get any from the
sea because the sea fish are of the same size with
those in Europe, and consequently not worth catch-
ing. Whereby it is manifest that nature, in the pro-
duction of plants and animals of so extraordinary a
bulk, is wholly confined to this continent. However,
now and then they take a whale that happens to be
dashed against the rocks, which the common people
feed on heartily. These whales I have known so large
that a man could hardly carry one upon his shoulders. And sometimes for curiosity they are brought
in hampers to Lorbrulgrud. I saw one of them in a
dish at the King's table, which passed for a rarity,
but I did not observe he was fond of it; for I think
indeed the bigness disgusted him, although I have
seen one somewhat larger in Greenland.

The country is well inhabited, for it contains fifty-one cities, near a hundred walled towns, and a great number of villages. Lorbrulgrud stands upon almost two equal parts on each side the river that passes through. It contains above eighty thousand houses and about six hundred thousand inhabitants. It is in length three *glonglungs* (which make about fifty-

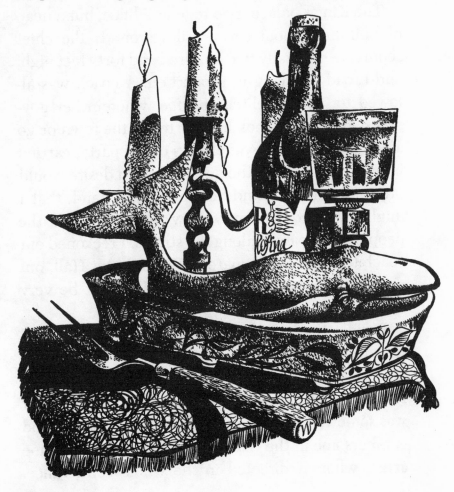

four English miles) and two and a half in breadth, as I measured it myself in the royal map made by the King's order, which was laid on the ground on purpose for me, and extended a hundred feet. I paced the diameter and circumference several times barefoot and, computing by the scale, measured it pretty exactly.

The King's palace is no regular edifice, but a heap of buildings about seven miles around: the chief rooms are generally two hundred and forty feet high, and broad and long in proportion. A coach was allowed to Glumdalclitch and me, wherein her governess frequently took her out to see the town or go among the shops. I was always of the party, carried in my box; although the girl at my own desire would often take me out, and hold me in her hand, that I might more conveniently view the houses and the people as we passed along the streets. I reckoned our coach to be about a square of Westminster Hall, but not altogether so high; however, I cannot be very exact.

Besides the large box in which I was usually carried, the Queen ordered a smaller one to be made for me, of about twelve feet square, and ten high, for the convenience of traveling, because the other was somewhat too large for Glumdalclitch's lap, and cumbersome in the coach. It was made by the same artist, whom I directed in the whole contrivance.

This traveling closet was an exact square with a window in the middle of three of the squares, and each window was latticed with iron wire on the outside, to prevent accidents in long journeys. On the fourth side, which had no window, two strong staples were fixed, through which the person that carried me, when I had a mind to be on horseback, put in a leathern belt, and buckled it about his waist. This was always the office of some grave trusty servant in whom I could confide, whether I attended the King and Queen in their progresses, or were disposed to see the gardens, or pay a visit to some great lady or minister of state in the court, when Glumdalclitch happened to be out of order. I soon began to be known and esteemed among the greatest officers, I suppose more upon account of their Majesties' favor than any merit of my own.

In journeys, when I was weary of the coach, a servant on horseback would buckle my box and place it on a cushion before him, and there I had a full prospect of the country on three sides from my three windows. I had in this closet a field bed and a hammock hung from the ceiling, two chairs and a table, neatly screwed to the floor, to prevent being tossed about by the agitation of the horse or the coach. And having been long used to sea voyages, those motions, although sometimes very violent, did not much discompose me.

Whenever I had a mind to see the town, it was always in my traveling closet, which Glumdalclitch held in her lap in a kind of open sedan, after the fashion of the country, borne by four men, and attended by two others in the Queen's livery. The people, who had often heard of me, were very curious to crowd about the sedan, and the girl was complaisant enough to make the bearers stop, and to take me in her hand that I might be more conveniently seen.

I was very desirous to see the chief temple, and particularly the tower belonging to it, which is reckoned the highest in the kingdom. Accordingly, one day my nurse carried me thither, but I may truly say I came back disappointed. For the height is not above three thousand feet, reckoning from the ground to the highest pinnacle top, which, allowing for the difference between the size of those people and us in Europe, is no great matter for admiration, nor at all equal in proportion (if I rightly remember) to Salisbury steeple. But, not to detract from a nation to which during my life I shall acknowledge myself extremely obliged, it must be allowed that whatever this famous tower wants in height is amply made up in beauty and strength. For the walls are near a hundred feet thick, built of hewn stone, whereof each is about forty feet square, and adorned on all sides with statues of gods and emperors cut in marble larger than the life, placed in their several niches. I measured a little finger which had fallen down from one of these statues, and lay unperceived among some rubbish, and found it exactly four feet and an inch in length. Glumdalclitch wrapped it up in a handkerchief, and carried it home in her pocket to keep among other trinkets, of which the girl was very fond, as children at her age usually are.

The King's kitchen is indeed a noble building, vaulted at top, and about six hundred feet high. The great oven is not so wide by ten yards as the cupola at St. Paul's, for I measured the latter on purpose after my return. But if I should describe the kitchen grate, the prodigious pots and kettles, the joints of meat turning on the spits, with many other particulars, perhaps I should be hardly believed.

His Majesty seldom keeps above six hundred horses in his stables; they are generally from fifty-four to sixty feet high. But when he goes abroad on solemn days he is attended for state by a militia guard of five hundred horse, which indeed I thought was the most splendid sight that could be ever beheld, till I saw part of his army in battalions.

I should have lived happily enough in that country if my littleness had not exposed me to several ridiculous and troublesome accidents, some of which I shall venture to relate.

Glumdalclitch often carried me into the gardens of the court in my smaller box, and would sometimes take me out of it and hold me in her hand or set me down to walk. I remember, before the dwarf left the Queen, he followed us one day into those gardens, and my nurse having set me down, he and I being close together, near some dwarf apple trees, I must needs show my wit by a silly allusion between him and the trees, which happens to hold in their language as it does in ours. Whereupon the malicious rogue, watching his opportunity, when I was walking under one of them, shook it directly over my head, by which a dozen apples, each of them near as large as a Bristol barrel, came tumbling about my ears. One of them hit me on the back as I chanced to stoop, and knocked me down flat on my face, but I received no other hurt, and the dwarf was pardoned at my desire.

Another day Glumdalclitch left me on a smooth grass plot to divert myself while she walked at some distance with her governess. In the meantime there suddenly fell such a violent shower of hail that I was immediately by the force of it struck to the ground, and when I was down, the hailstones gave me such cruel bangs all over the body as if I had been pelted with tennis balls. However, I made a shift to creep on all fours, and shelter myself by lying flat on my face on the lee side of a border of lemon thyme, but so bruised from head to foot that I could not go abroad in ten days. Neither is this at all to be wondered at because in that country a hailstone is near eighteen hundred times as large as one in Europe, which I can assert upon experience, having been so curious as to weigh and measure them.

But a more dangerous accident happened to me in the same garden, when my little nurse believing she had put me in a secure place, which I often entreated her to do, that I might enjoy my own thoughts, and having left my box at home to avoid the trouble of carrying it, went to another part of the garden with her governess and some ladies of her acquaintance.

While she was absent and out of hearing, a small white spaniel belonging to one of the chief gardeners, having got by accident into the garden, happened to range near the place where I lay. The dog, following the scent, came directly up, and taking me in his mouth, ran straight to his master, wagging his tail, and set me gently on the ground. By good fortune he had been so well taught that I was carried between his teeth without the least hurt, or even tearing my clothes.

But the poor gardener, who knew me well and had a great kindness for me, was in a terrible fright. He gently took me up in both his hands and asked me how I did. But I was so amazed and out of breath that I could not speak a word. In a few minutes I came to myself, and he carried me safe to my little nurse, who by this time had returned to the place where she left me and was in cruel agonies when I did not appear, nor answer when she called. She severely reprimanded the gardener on account of his dog. But the thing was hushed up, and never known at court; for the girl was afraid of the Queen's anger and truly, as to myself, I thought it would not be for my reputation that such a story should go about.

In this manner I had several conversations with him

[SEE PAGE 160]

This accident absolutely determined Glumdal-clitch never to trust me abroad out of her sight. I had been long afraid of this resolution, and therefore concealed from her some little unlucky adventures that happened in those times when I was left by myself. Once a hawk hovering over the garden made a swoop at me, and if I had not resolutely drawn my sword, and run under a thick trellis, he would have certainly carried me away in his claws. Another time, walking to the top of a fresh molehill, I fell to my neck in the hole through which that animal had cast up the earth. I coined some lie, not worth remembering, to excuse myself for spoiling my clothes. I likewise broke my right shin against the shell of a snail, which I happened to stumble over, as I was walking alone and thinking on poor England.

I cannot tell whether I was more pleased or mortified to observe in those solitary walks that the smaller birds did not appear to be at all afraid of me, but would hop about within a yard's distance, looking for worms and other food with as much indifference and security as if no creature at all were near them. I remember a thrush had the confidence to snatch out of my hand with his bill a piece of cake that Glumdalclitch had just given me for my breakfast. When I attempted to catch any of these birds, they would boldly turn against me, endeavoring to pick my fingers, which I dared not venture within

their reach. And then they would hop back uncon-
cerned to hunt for worms or snails, as they did before. But one day I took a thick cudgel, and threw
it with all my strength so luckily at a linnet that I
knocked him down, and seizing him by the neck with
both my hands, ran with him in triumph to my nurse.
However, the bird, who had only been stunned, recovered himself and gave me so many boxes with his
wings on both sides of my head and body, though I
held him at arm's length, and was out of the reach of
his claws, that I was twenty times thinking to let him
go. But I was soon relieved by one of our servants,
who wrung off the bird's neck, and I had him next

day for dinner, by the Queen's command. This linnet, as near as I can remember, seemed to be somewhat larger than an English swan.

The Queen, who often used to hear me talk of my
sea voyages, and took all occasions to divert me
when I was melancholy, asked me whether I understood how to handle a sail or an oar, and whether a
little exercise of rowing might not be convenient for
my health. I answered that I understood both very
well. For, although my proper employment had been
to be surgeon or doctor to the ship, yet often, upon a
pinch, I was forced to work like a common mariner.
But I could not see how this could be done in their
country, where the smallest wherry was equal to a
first-rate man-of-war among us, and such a boat as I
could manage would never live in any of their rivers.
Her Majesty said, if I would contrive a boat, her own
joiner should make it and she would provide a place
for me to sail in.

The fellow was an ingenious workman, and by my
instructions in ten days finished a pleasure boat with
all its tackling, able conveniently to hold eight Europeans. When it was finished, the Queen was so delighted that she ran with it in her lap to the King,
who ordered it to be put in a cistern full of water
where I could not manage my two sculls, or little
oars, for want of room. But the Queen had before
contrived another project. She ordered the joiner to

make a wooden trough of three hundred feet long, fifty broad, and eight deep; which, being well pitched to prevent leaking, was placed on the floor along the wall, in an outer room of the palace. It had a cock near the bottom to let out the water when it began to grow stale, and two servants could easily fill it in half an hour.

Here I often used to row for my own diversion, as well as that of the Queen and her ladies, who thought themselves well entertained with my skill and agility. Sometimes I would put up my sail, and then my business was only to steer, while the ladies gave me a gale with their fans. And when they were weary, some of the pages would blow my sail forward with their breath, while I showed my art by steering starboard or larboard as I pleased. When I had done, Glumdalclitch always carried my boat into her closet, and hung it on a nail to dry.

In this exercise I once met an accident which had like to have cost me my life. One of the pages having put my boat into the trough, the governess who attended Glumdalclitch very officiously lifted me up to place me in the boat, but I happened to slip through her fingers and should have fallen down forty feet upon the floor if by the luckiest chance in the world I had not been stopped by a large pin that stuck in the good gentlewoman's stomacher. The head of the pin passed between my shirt and the waistband of

my breeches, and thus I was held by the middle in the air till Glumdalclitch ran to my relief.

Another time, one of the servants, whose office it was to fill my trough every third day with fresh water, was so careless to let a huge frog slip out of his pail. The frog lay concealed till I was put into my boat, but then seeking a resting place, climbed up, and made it lean so much on one side that I was forced to balance it with all my weight on the other to prevent overturning. When the frog got in, it hopped at once half the length of the boat, and then over my head, backward and forward. The largeness of its features made it appear the most deformed animal that can be conceived. However, I desired

Glumdalclitch to let me deal with it alone. I banged it a good while with one of my sculls, and at last forced it to leap out of the boat.

But the greatest danger I ever underwent in that kingdom was from a monkey, who belonged to one of the clerks of the kitchen. Glumdalclitch had locked me up in her closet, while she went somewhere upon business or a visit. The weather being very warm, the closet window was left open, as well as the windows and the door of my bigger box, in which I usually lived. As I sat quietly meditating at my table, I heard something bounce in at the closet window and skip about from one side to the other; whereat, although I was much alarmed, yet I ventured to look out, but stirred not from my seat. And then I saw this frolicsome animal, frisking and leaping up and down, till at last he came to my box, which he seemed to view with great pleasure and curiosity, peeping in at the door and every window. I retreated to the farther corner of my room, or box, but the monkey put me into such a fright that I wanted presence of mind to conceal myself under the bed, as I might easily have done. After some time spent in peeping, grinning, and chattering, he at last espied me, and reaching one of his paws in at the door, as a cat does when she plays with a mouse, although I often shifted place to avoid him, he at length seized the lappet of my coat and dragged me out.

He took me up in his right forefoot just as I have seen the same sort of creature do with a kitten in Europe. And when I offered to struggle, he squeezed me so hard that I thought it more prudent to submit. I have good reason to believe that he took me for a young one of his own species, by his often stroking my face very gently with his other paw. In these diversions he was interrupted by a noise at the closet door, as if somebody were opening it. Whereupon he suddenly leaped up to the window at which he had come in, and thence upon the leads and gutters, walking upon three legs, and holding me in the fourth, till he clambered up to a roof that was next to ours.

I heard Glumdalclitch give a shriek at the moment he was carrying me out. The poor girl was almost distracted. That quarter of the palace was all in an uproar. The servants ran for ladders. The monkey was seen by hundreds in the court, sitting upon the ridge of a building, holding me like a baby in one of his forepaws, and feeding me with the other, by cramming into my mouth some victuals he had squeezed out of the bag on one side of his chaps, and patting me when I would not eat. Many of the rabble below could not forbear laughing at this, neither do I think they justly ought to be blamed, for without question the sight was ridiculous enough to everybody but myself. Some of the people threw up stones, hoping

to drive the monkey down; but this was strictly forbidden, or else very probably my brains had been
dashed out.

The ladders were now applied, and mounted by
several men. The monkey, observing this and not
being able to make speed enough with his three legs,
let me drop on a ridge tile and made his escape. Here
I sat for some time three hundred yards from the
ground, expecting every moment to be blown down
by the wind, or to fall by my own giddiness, and
come tumbling over and over from the ridge to the
eaves. But an honest lad, one of my nurse's footmen,
climbed up, and putting me into his breeches pocket,
brought me down safe.

I was so weak and bruised in the sides with the
squeezes given me by this odious animal that I was
forced to keep my bed a fortnight. The King, Queen,
and all the court sent every day to inquire after my
health, and her Majesty made me several visits during my sickness. The monkey was killed, and an order issued that no such animal should be kept about
the palace.

When I attended the King after my recovery, to
return him thanks for his favors, he was pleased to
rally me a good deal upon this adventure. He asked
me what my thoughts and speculations were while I
lay in the monkey's paw, how I liked the victuals he
gave me, his manner of feeding, and whether the

fresh air on the roof had sharpened my appetite. He desired to know what I would have done upon such an occasion in my own country. I told his Majesty that in Europe we had no monkeys, except such as were brought for curiosities from other places, and so small that I could deal with a dozen of them together if they presumed to attack me. And as for that monstrous animal with whom I was so lately engaged (it was indeed as large as an elephant), if my fears had suffered me to think so far as to make use of my sword (looking fiercely and clapping my hand upon the hilt as I spoke) when he poked his paw into my chamber, perhaps I should have given him such a wound as would have made him glad to withdraw it with more haste than he put it in. This I delivered in a firm tone, like a person who was jealous lest his courage be called in question. However, my speech produced nothing but loud laughter, which all the respect due to his Majesty from those about him could not make them contain. This made me reflect how vain an attempt it is for a man to endeavor doing himself honor among those who are out of all degree of equality or comparison with him. Frequently, in England, a contemptible varlet, without the least title to birth, person, wit, or common sense, shall presume to look with importance, and put himself upon a foot with the greatest persons of the kingdom.

CHAPTER 13

Gulliver Amuses the
King and Queen

THE KING had frequent concerts at court, to which I was sometimes carried, and set in my box on a table to hear them. But the noise was so great that I could hardly distinguish the tunes. I am confident that all the drums and trumpets of a royal army, beating and sounding together just at your ears, could not equal it. My practice was to have my box removed as far as I could from the places where the performers sat, then to shut the doors and windows, and draw the window curtains; after which I found their music not disagreeable.

I had learned in my youth to play a little upon the spinet. Glumdalclitch kept one in her chamber, and a master attended twice a week to teach her. I call it a spinet, because it somewhat resembled that instrument and was played upon in the same manner. A

fancy came into my head that I would entertain the King and Queen with an English tune upon this instrument. But this appeared extremely difficult; for the spinet was near sixty feet long, each key being almost a foot wide, so that, with my arms extended, I could not reach to above five keys, and to press them down required a good smart stroke with my fist, which would be too great a labor, and to no purpose. The method I contrived was this:

I prepared two round sticks about the bigness of common cudgels. They were thicker at one end than the other, and I covered the thicker ends with a piece of a mouse's skin, so that by rapping on them I might neither damage the tops of the keys nor interrupt the sound. Before the spinet a bench was placed, about four feet below the keys, and I was put upon the bench. I ran sidling upon it that way and this, as fast as I could, banging the proper keys with my two sticks, and made a shift to play a jig, to the great satisfaction of both their Majesties. It was the most violent exercise I ever underwent, and yet I could not strike above sixteen keys, nor, consequently, play the bass and treble together, as other artists do; which was a great disadvantage to my performance.

The King, who, as I before observed, was a prince of excellent understanding, would frequently order that I should be brought in my box and set upon the table in his room. He would then command me to bring one of my chairs out of the box, and sit down within three yards' distance upon the top of the cabinet, which brought me almost to a level with his face. In this manner I had several conversations with him. I one day took the freedom to tell his Majesty that the contempt he showed toward Europe, and the rest of the world, did not seem answerable to those excellent qualities of the mind he was master of. That reason did not extend itself with the bulk of the body; on the contrary, we observed in our country that the tallest persons were usually least provided with it. That among other animals, bees and ants had the reputation of more industry, art and sagacity, than many of the larger kinds. And that, inconsiderable as he took me to be, I hoped I might live to do his Majesty some signal service. The King heard me with attention, and began to conceive a much better opinion of me than he had ever before. He desired I would give him as exact an account of the government of England as I possibly could; because, fond as princes commonly are of their own customs, he should be glad to hear of anything that might deserve imitation.

I began my discourse by informing his Majesty that our dominions consisted of two islands, which composed three mighty kingdoms under one sovereign, besides our plantations in America. I dwelt long upon the fertility of our soil and the temperature of our climate. I then spoke at large upon the constitution of an English Parliament, partly made up of an illustrious body called the House of Peers, persons of the noblest blood, and of the most ancient and ample patrimonies.

I described that extraordinary care always taken of their education in arts and arms, to qualify them for being counselors born to the king and kingdom, to have a share in the legislature, to be members of the highest court, whence there could be no appeal, and to be champions always ready for the defense of their prince and country, by their valor, conduct, and fidelity. That these were the ornament and bulwark of the kingdom, worthy followers of their most renowned ancestors, whose honor had been the re-

ward of their virtue, from which their posterity were
never once known to degenerate. To these were
joined several holy persons, as part of that assembly,
under the title of bishops, whose peculiar business it
is to take care of religion, and of those who instruct
the people therein.

The other part of Parliament consisted of an assembly called the House of Commons, who were all
principal gentlemen, freely picked and culled out by
the people themselves, for their great abilities and
love of their country, to represent the wisdom of the
whole nation. And these two bodies make up the
most august assembly in Europe, to whom, in conjunction with the prince, the whole legislature is
committed.

I then descended to the courts of justice, over
which the judges, those venerable sages and inter-
preters of the law, presided, for determining the
disputed rights and properties of men, as well as for
the punishment of vice and the protection of innocence. I mentioned the prudent management of our
treasury; the valor and achievements of our forces
by sea and land. I computed the number of our
people, by reckoning how many millions there might
be of each religious sect or political party among us.
I did not omit even our sports and pastimes, or any
other particular which I thought might redound to
the honor of my country. And I finished all with a

brief historical account of affairs and events in England for about a hundred years past.

This conversation was not ended under five audiences, each of several hours, and the King heard the whole with great attention, frequently taking notes of what I spoke, as well as memorandums of several questions he intended to ask me.

When I had put an end to these long discourses, his Majesty in a sixth audience, consulting his notes, proposed many doubts, queries, and objections upon every article. He asked what methods were used to cultivate the minds and bodies of our young nobility, and in what kind of business they commonly spent the first and teachable part of their lives; what course was taken to supply that assembly when any noble family became extinct; what qualifications were necessary in those who were to be created new lords; whether the humor of the prince, a sum of money to a court lady or a prime minister, or a design of strengthening a party opposite to the public interest, ever happened to be motives in those advancements; what share of knowledge these lords had in the laws of their country; whether they were always so free from avarice that they would not accept a bribe.

He then desired to know what arts were practiced in electing those whom I called commoners; whether a stranger with a strong purse might not influence the vulgar voters to choose him before their own landlord, or the most considerable gentleman in the neighborhood; how it came to pass that people were so violently bent upon getting into this assembly, without any salary or pension. This appeared such an exalted strain of public spirit that his Majesty seemed to doubt it might possibly not be always sincere.

Upon what I said in relation to our courts of justice, his Majesty desired to be satisfied in several points. And this I was the better able to do, having been formerly almost ruined by a long suit in chancery, which was decreed for me with costs. He asked what time was usually spent in determining between right and wrong, and what degree of expense; whether advocates and orators had liberty to plead in causes manifestly known to be unjust, vexatious, or oppressive; whether party, in religion or politics, was observed to be of any weight in the scale of justice.

He was amazed to hear me talk of such serious and expensive wars: that certainly we must be a quarrelsome people, or live among very bad neighbors, and that our generals must needs be richer than our kings. He asked what business we had out of our own islands, unless upon the score of trade or treaty or to defend the coasts with our fleet. Above all, he was amazed to hear me talk of a mercenary standing army in the midst of peace, and among a free people. He said, if we were governed by our own consent in the persons of our representatives, he could not imagine of whom we were afraid, or against whom we were to fight. And he would like my opinion, whether a private man's house might not better be defended by himself, his children, and his family than by half a dozen rascals picked up at a venture in the streets, for small wages, who might get a hundred times more by cutting their throats.

He observed that among the diversions of our nobility and gentry I had mentioned gaming. He desired to know at what age this entertainment was usually taken up, and when it was laid down; how much of their time it employed; whether it ever went so high as to affect their fortunes; whether mean, vicious people, by their dexterity in that art, might not arrive at great riches, and sometimes keep our very nobles in dependence, as well as habituate them to vile companions, wholly take them from the improvement of their minds, and force them, by the losses they have received, to learn and practice that infamous dexterity upon others.

His Majesty in another audience was at pains to recapitulate the sum of all I had spoken. He compared the questions he made with the answers I had given, then taking me into his hands, and stroking me gently, delivered himself in these words, which I shall never forget nor the manner he spoke them in: "My little friend Grildrig, you have made a most admirable panegyric upon your country; you have

clearly proved that ignorance, idleness, and vice may
be sometimes the only ingredients for qualifying a
legislator; that laws are best explained, interpreted,
and applied by those whose interest and abilities lie
in perverting, confounding, and eluding them. I observe among you some lines of an institution, which
in its original might have been tolerable, but these
half erased, and the rest wholly blurred and blotted
by corruptions. It does not appear, from all you have
said, how any one virtue is required toward the pro-
curement of any one station among you; much less
that men are ennobled on account of their virtue,
that priests are advanced for their piety or learning,
soldiers for their conduct or valor, judges for their
integrity, senators for the love of their country, or
counselors for their wisdom. As for yourself," continued the King, "who have spent the greatest part
of your life in traveling, I am well disposed to hope
you may hitherto have escaped many vices of your
country. But by what I have gathered from your own
relation, and the answers I have with much pains
wrung and extorted from you, I cannot but conclude
the bulk of your natives to be the most pernicious
race of little odious vermin that nature ever suffered
to crawl upon the surface of the earth."

Nothing but an extreme love of truth could have
hindered me from concealing this part of my story. It
was in vain to show my resentments, which were al-

ways turned into ridicule; and I was forced to rest with patience while my noble and most beloved country was so injuriously treated. But this prince happened to be so curious and inquisitive upon every particular, that it could not consist with either gratitude or good manners to refuse giving him what satisfaction I was able. Yet thus much I may be allowed to say in my own vindication, that I artfully eluded many of his questions and gave to every point a more favorable turn than the strictness of truth would allow. I would hide the frailties and deformities of my political mother, and place her virtues and beauties in the most advantageous light. This was my sincere endeavor in those many discourses I had with that mighty monarch, although it unfortunately failed of success.

But great allowances should be made for a King who lives wholly secluded from the rest of the world, and must therefore be altogether unacquainted with the manners and customs that most prevail in other nations. The want of this knowledge will ever produce many prejudices, and a certain narrowness of thinking. And it would be hard, indeed, if so remote a prince's notions of virtue and vice were to be offered as a standard for all mankind.

To confirm what I have now said and, further, to show the miserable effects of a confined education, I shall here insert a passage which will hardly obtain belief. In the hope of ingratiating myself further into his Majesty's favor, I told him of an invention discovered between three and four hundred years ago —the uses of gunpowder. A proper quantity of this powder rammed into a hollow tube of brass or iron would drive a ball of iron or lead with such violence and speed that nothing was able to sustain its force. The largest balls would not only destroy whole ranks of an army, but batter the strongest walls to the ground, sink down ships to the bottom of the sea; and, when linked together by a chain, would cut through masts and rigging and lay all waste before them. That this powder put into large hollow balls of iron and discharged by an engine into some city would rip up the pavements, tear the houses to pieces, burst and throw splinters on every side, and kill all who came near.

The King was struck with horror at the description I had given of those terrible engines. He was amazed how so impotent and groveling an insect as I (these were his expressions) could entertain such inhuman ideas, and in so familiar a manner as to appear wholly unmoved at all the scenes of blood and desolation, which I had painted as the common effects of those destructive machines, whereof he said some evil genius, enemy to mankind, must have been the first contriver. As for himself, he protested that, although few things delighted him so much as new discoveries in art or in nature, he would rather lose half his king-

dom than be privy to such a secret, which he commanded me, as I valued my life, never to mention any more.

I remember very well, in a discourse one day with the King, when I happened to say there were several thousand books among us written upon the art of government, it gave him a very mean opinion of our understandings. He could not tell what I meant by secrets of state, where an enemy or some rival nation was not in the case. And he gave it for his opinion, that whoever could make two ears of corn or two blades of grass to grow upon a spot of ground where only one grew before would deserve better of mankind and do more essential service to his country than the whole race of politicians put together.

The learning of this people is very defective, consisting only in morality, history, poetry, and mathematics, wherein they must be allowed to excel. But
the last of these is wholly applied to what may be
useful in life, to the improvement of agriculture, and
all mechanical arts; so that among us it would be
little esteemed.

No law of that country must exceed in words the
number of letters in their alphabet, which consists
of only twenty-two. But indeed few of them extend
even to that length, and they are expressed in the
most plain and simple terms.

They, as well as the Chinese, have had the art of
printing time out of mind. But their libraries are not
very large. That of the King, which is reckoned the
biggest, does not amount to above a thousand volumes, placed in a gallery twelve hundred feet long,
from which I had liberty to borrow what books I
pleased. The Queen's joiner had contrived in one of
Glumdalclitch's rooms a kind of wooden machine
twenty-five feet high, formed like a standing ladder.
The steps were each fifty feet long. It was indeed a
movable pair of stairs, the lowest end placed at ten
feet distance from the wall of the chamber.

The book I had a mind to read was put up leaning
against the wall. I first mounted to the upper step of
the ladder, and turning my face toward the book,
began at the top of the page, and so walking to the

right and left about eight or ten yards, according to the length of the lines, till I had got a little below the level of my eyes, and then descending gradually till I came to the bottom; after which I mounted again and began the other page in the same manner, and so turned over the leaf, which I could easily do with both my hands, for it was as thick and stiff as pasteboard, and in the largest folios not above eighteen or twenty feet long.

CHAPTER 14

Gulliver Returns

to England

I HAD ALWAYS A STRONG IMPULSE that I should some time recover my liberty, though it was impossible to conjecture by what means or to form any project with the least hope of succeeding. The ship in which I sailed was the first ever known to be driven within sight of that coast, and the King had given strict orders that if at any time another appeared it should be taken ashore, and all its crew and passengers brought to Lorbrulgrud.

Meanwhile I was, indeed, treated with much kindness. I was the favorite of a great King and Queen, and the delight of the whole court, but it was upon such a foot as ill became the dignity of human kind. I could never forget those domestic pledges I had left behind me. I wanted to be among people with whom I could converse upon even terms, and walk about the streets and fields without fear of being trod to death like a frog or a young puppy. But my deliverance came sooner than I expected, and in a manner not very common; the whole story and circumstances of which I shall faithfully relate.

I had now been two years in this country; and about the beginning of the third, Glumdalclitch and I attended the King and Queen in a progress to the south coast. I was carried, as usual, in my traveling box, which, as I have already described, was a very convenient closet twelve feet wide. And I had ordered a hammock to be fixed by silken ropes from the four corners at the top, to break the jolts, when a servant carried me before him on horseback, as I sometimes desired, and would often sleep in my hammock while we were upon the road. On the roof of my closet, just over the middle of the hammock, I ordered the joiner to cut out a hole a foot square, to give me air in hot weather as I slept, which hole I shut at pleasure with a board that drew backward and forward through a groove.

When we came to our journey's end, the King thought proper to pass a few days at a palace he has near Flanflasnic, a city within eighteen English miles of the seaside. Glumdalclitch and I were much fatigued. I had got a small cold, but the poor girl was so ill as to be confined to her chamber. I longed to see the ocean, which must be the only scene of my escape, if ever it should happen. I pretended to be

worse than I really was, and desired leave to take the
fresh air of the sea, with a page whom I was very
fond of and who had sometimes been trusted with
me. I shall never forget with what unwillingness
Glumdalclitch consented, nor the strict charge she
gave the page to be careful of me, bursting at the
same time into a flood of tears as if she had some
foreboding of what was to happen.

The boy took me out in my box about half an
hour's walk from the palace, toward the rocks on the
seashore. I ordered him to set me down, and lifting
up one of my sashes, cast many a wistful, melancholy
look toward the sea. I found myself not very well,
and told the page that I had a mind to take a nap in
my hammock, which I hoped would do me good. I
got in, and the boy shut the window close down to
keep out the cold.

I soon fell asleep, and all I can conjecture is that
while I slept the page, thinking no danger could
happen, went among the rocks to look for birds' eggs,
having before observed him from my window search-
ing about, and picking up one or two in the clefts. Be
that as it will, I found myself suddenly awaked with
a violent pull upon the ring which was fastened at
the top of my box for the convenience of carriage. I
felt my box raised very high in the air, and then
borne forward with prodigious speed. The first jolt
had like to have shaken me out of my hammock, but

afterward the motion was easy enough. I called out several times as loud as I could raise my voice, but all to no purpose. I looked toward my windows and could see nothing but the clouds and sky.

I heard a noise just over my head like the beating of wings, and then began to perceive the woeful condition I was in. Some eagle had got the ring of my box in his beak, with an intent to let it fall on a rock like a tortoise in a shell, and then pick out my body, and devour it.

In a little time I observed the noise of the flutter of wings to increase very fast, and my box was tossed up and down, like a signpost on a windy day. I heard several bangs or buffets, as I thought, given to the eagle and then all of a sudden felt myself falling perpendicularly down for above a minute, but with such incredible swiftness that I almost lost my breath. My fall was stopped by a terrible squash, that sounded louder to my ears than the cataract of Niagara. After that I was quite in the dark for another minute, and then my box began to rise so high that I could see light from the tops of my windows. I now perceived that i had fallen into the sea.

My box, by the weight of my body, the goods that were in it, and the broad plates of iron fixed for strength at the four corners of the top and bottom, floated five feet deep in water. I did then, and do now, suppose that the eagle which flew away with my box was pursued by two or three others, and forced to let me drop while he was defending himself against the rest, who hoped to share in the prey.

The plates of iron fastened at the bottom of the box preserved the balance while it fell, and hindered it from being broken on the surface of the water. Every joint of it was well grooved, and the door did not move on hinges, but up and down like a sash, which kept my closet so tight that very little water came in. I got with much difficulty out of my hammock, having first ventured to draw back the slipboard on the roof already mentioned, contrived on purpose to let in air, for want of which I found myself almost stifled.

How often did I then wish myself with my dear Glumdalclitch, from whom one single hour had so far divided me! And I may say with truth that in the midst of my own misfortunes I could not forbear lamenting my poor nurse, the grief she would suffer for my loss, the displeasure of the Queen, and the ruin of her fortune. Perhaps many travelers have not been under greater difficulties and distress than I was at this juncture, expecting every moment to see my box dashed in pieces, or at least overset by the first violent blast or a rising wave.

A breach in one single pane of glass would have been immediate death: nor could anything have preserved the windows, but the strong lattice wires placed on the outside against accidents in traveling. I saw the water ooze in at several crannies, although the leaks were not considerable, and I endeavored to stop them as well as I could. I was not able to lift up the roof, which otherwise I certainly should have done and sat on the top of it, where I might at least preserve myself some hours longer than by being shut up, as I may call it, in the hold. Or, if I escaped these dangers for a day or two, what could I expect but a miserable death from cold and hunger! I was four hours under these circumstances, expecting and indeed wishing every moment to be my last.

I have already told the reader that there were two strong staples fixed upon that side of my box which had no window, and into which the servant who used to carry me on horseback would put a leathern belt, and buckle it about his waist. Being in this disconsolate state, I heard or at least thought I heard some kind of grating noise on that side of my box where the staples were fixed, and soon after I began to fancy that the box was pulled or towed along in the sea; for I now and then felt a sort of tugging, which made the waves rise near the tops of my windows, leaving me almost in the dark. This gave me some faint hopes of relief, although I was not able to imagine how it could be brought about.

I ventured to unscrew one of my chairs, which were always fastened to the floor; and having made a hard shift to screw it down again directly under the slipping board that I had lately opened, I mounted on the chair, and putting my mouth as near as I could to the hole, I called for help in a loud voice, and in all the languages I understood. I then fastened my handkerchief to a stick I usually carried, and thrusting it up the hole, waved it several times in the air, so that if any boat or ship were near, the seamen

might conjecture some unhappy mortal to be shut up in the box.

I found no effect from all I could do, but plainly perceived myself to be moved along. And in the space of an hour, or better, that side of the box where the staples were, and had no window, struck against something that was hard. I apprehended it to be a rock, and found myself tossed more than ever. I plainly heard a noise upon the cover of my closet, like that of a cable, and the grating of it as it passed through the ring. I then found myself hoisted up by degrees at least three feet higher than I was before. Whereupon I again thrust up my stick and handkerchief, calling for help till I was almost hoarse. In return to which I heard a great shout repeated three times, giving me such transports of joy as are not to be conceived but by those who feel them.

I now heard a trampling over my head, and somebody calling through a hole with a loud voice in the English tongue: "If there be anybody below, let them speak." I answered that I was an Englishman, drawn by ill fortune into the greatest calamity that ever any creature underwent, and begged, by all that is moving, to be delivered out of the dungeon I was in. The voice replied that I was safe, for my box was fastened to their ship; and the carpenter should immediately come and saw an hole in the cover, large enough to pull me out. I said that was needless and would take up too much time, for there was no more to be done, but let one of the crew put his finger into the ring, and take the box out of the sea into the ship, and so into the captain's cabin. Some of them, upon hearing me talk so wildly, thought I was mad; others laughed. It never came into my head that I was now among people of my own stature and strength.

The carpenter came, and in a few minutes sawed a passage about four feet square, then let down a small ladder, upon which I mounted, and from thence was taken into the ship in a very weak condition.

The sailors were all in amazement and asked me a thousand questions, which I had no inclination to answer. I was equally confounded at the sight of so many pygmies, for such I took them to be, after having so long accustomed my eyes to the monstrous objects I had left. But the captain, Mr. Thomas Wilcocks, an honest, worthy Shropshire man, observing I was ready to faint, took me into his cabin, gave me a cordial to comfort me, and made me turn in upon his own bed, advising me to take a little rest, of which I had great need.

Before I went to sleep I gave him to understand that I had some valuable furniture in my box, too good to be lost, a fine hammock, a handsome field bed, two chairs, a table, and a cabinet; that my closet was hung on all sides, or rather quilted, with silk and cotton; that if he would let one of the crew bring my closet into his cabin, I would open it there before him, and show him my goods. The captain, hearing me utter these absurdities, concluded I was raving. However (I suppose to pacify me), he promised to give order as I desired, and going upon deck sent some of his men down into my closet whence (as I afterward found) they drew up all my goods, and stripped off the quilting; but the chairs, cabinet, and bedstead, being screwed to the floor, were much damaged by the ignorance of the seamen, who tore them up by force. Then they knocked off some of the boards for the use of the ship, and when they had got all they had a mind for, let the hull drop into the sea, which by reason of many breaches made in the bottom and sides, sank at once. And indeed I was glad not to have been a spectator of the havoc they made; because I am confident it would have sensibly touched me, by bringing former passages into my mind, which I had rather forget.

I slept some hours, but perpetually disturbed with dreams of the place I had left, and the dangers I had escaped. However, upon waking I found myself much recovered. It was now about eight o'clock at night, and the captain ordered supper immediately, thinking I had already fasted too long. He entertained me with great kindness, observing me not to look wildly or talk inconsistently. And when we were left alone, he desired I would give him a relation of my travels, and by what accident I came to be set adrift in that monstrous wooden chest.

He said that about twelve o'clock at noon, as he was looking through his glass, he spied it at a distance, and thought it was a sail. Upon coming nearer, and finding his error, he sent out his longboat to discover what it was; but his men came back in a fright, swearing they had seen a swimming house. He laughed at their folly, and went himself in the boat, ordering his men to take a strong cable along with them. The weather being calm, he rowed round me several times, observed my windows, and the wire lattices that defended them, and he discovered two staples upon one side, which was all of boards without any passage for light. He then commanded his men to row up to that side, and fastening a cable to one of the staples, ordered them to tow my chest (as he called it) toward the ship.

When it was there, he gave directions to fasten another cable to the ring fixed in the cover, and to raise up my chest with pulley, which all the sailors were not able to do above two or three feet. He said they saw my stick and handkerchief thrust out of the hole, and concluded that some unhappy men must be shut up in the cavity. I asked whether he or the crew had seen any prodigious birds in the air about the time he first discovered me. To this he answered that, discussing this matter with the sailors while I was asleep, one of them said he had observed three eagles flying toward the north, but remarked nothing of their being larger than the usual size, which I suppose must be imputed to the great height they were flying. He could not guess the reason of my question.

I then asked the captain how far he reckoned we might be from land. He said, by the best computation he could make, we were at least a hundred leagues. I assured him that he must be mistaken by almost half, for I had not left the country from where

I came above two hours before I dropped into the sea. Whereupon he began again to think that my brain was disturbed, of which he gave me a hint and advised me to go to bed in a cabin he had provided. I assured him I was well refreshed with his good entertainment and company, and as much in my senses as ever I was in my life.

He then grew serious, and desired to ask me freely whether I were not troubled in mind by the consciousness of some enormous crime, for which I was punished at the command of some prince, by exposing me in that chest, as great criminals in other countries have been forced to sea in a leaky vessel without provisions. Although he should be sorry to have taken so ill a man into his ship, yet he would engage his word to set me safe on shore in the first port where we arrived. He added that his suspicions were much increased by some very absurd speeches I had delivered at first to the sailors, and afterward to himself, in relation to my closet, or chest, as well as by my odd looks and behavior while I was at supper.

I begged his patience to hear me tell my story, which I faithfully did from the last time I left England to the moment he first discovered me. And as truth always forces its way into rational minds, so this honest, worthy gentleman, who had some tincture of learning and very good sense, was immediately convinced of my candor and veracity. But further to confirm all I had said, I entreated him to give order that my cabinet should be brought, of which I had the key in my pocket. I opened it in his presence and showed him the small collection of rarities I made in the country from where I had been so strangely delivered.

There was a collection of needles and pins from a foot to half a yard long; four wasp stings, like joiners' tacks; a lock of the Queen's hair; a gold ring which one day she made me a present of in a most obliging manner, taking it from her little finger, and throwing it over my head like a collar. I desired the captain would please to accept this ring in return of his civilities, which he absolutely refused. Lastly, I showed him the breeches I had then on, which were made of a mouse's skin.

He said he wondered at one thing very much, which was to hear me speak so loud, asking me whether the King or Queen of that country were hard of hearing. I told him it was what I had been used to for above two years past, and that I wondered as much at the voices of him and his men, who seemed to me only to whisper, and yet I could hear them well enough. But when I spoke in that country, it was like a man talking in the street to another looking out from the top of a steeple, unless when I was placed on a table or held in any person's hand. I told him I had likewise observed another thing, that when

I first got into the ship, and the sailors stood all about me, I thought they were the most little contemptible creatures I had ever beheld. For, indeed, while I was in that prince's country, I could never endure to look in a glass after my eyes had been accustomed to such prodigious objects, because the comparison gave me so despicable an opinion of myself.

The captain said that while we were at supper he observed me look at everything with a sort of wonder, and that I often seemed hardly able to contain my laughter, which he knew not well how to take, but imputed it to some disorder in my brain. I answered that it was very true; and I wondered how I could forbear, when I saw his dishes of the size of a silver threepence, a leg of pork hardly a mouthful, a cup not so big as a nutshell. And so I went on, describing the rest of his household stuff and provisions after the same manner. For, although the Queen had ordered a little equipage of all things necessary for me while I was in her service, yet my ideas were wholly taken up with what I saw on every side of me, and I winked at my own littleness as people do at their own faults.

Our voyage to England was very prosperous, but I shall not trouble the reader with a journal of it. The captain called in at one or two ports, and sent in his longboat for provisions and fresh water, but I never went out of the ship till we came into the Downs,

which was on the 3rd of June, 1706, about nine months after my escape. I offered to leave my goods in security for payment of my passage, but the captain protested he would not receive one farthing. We took kind leave of each other, and I made him promise he would come to see me at my house in Redriff. I hired a horse and guide for five shillings, which I borrowed of the captain.

As I was on the road, observing the littleness of the houses, the trees, the cattle, and the people, I began to think myself in Lilliput. I was afraid of trampling on every traveler I met, and often called aloud to have them stand out of the way, so that I had like to have got one or two broken heads for my impertinence.

When I came to my own house, for which I was forced to inquire, one of the servants opening the door, I bent down to go in (like a goose under a gate) for fear of striking my head. My wife ran out to embrace me, but I stooped lower than her knees, thinking she could otherwise never be able to reach my mouth. My daughter kneeled to ask my blessing, but I could not see her till she arose, having been so long used to stand with my head and eyes erect to above sixty feet; and then I went to take her up with one hand, by the waist. I looked down upon the servants and one or two friends who were in the house, as if they had been pygmies and I a giant. I told my wife she had been too thrifty, for I found she had starved herself and her daughter to nothing. In short, I behaved myself so unaccountably that they were all of the captain's opinion when he first saw me, and concluded I had lost my wits. This I mention as an instance of the great power of habit and prejudice.

In a little time, I and my family and friends came to a right understanding, but my wife protested I should never go to sea any more. Although my evil destiny so ordered that she had not power to hinder me.

Gulliver's Travels

PART III

Voyages to Laputa and the Country of the Houyhnhnms

CHAPTER 15

A Flying Island

I HAD NOT BEEN AT HOME above ten days, when Captain William Robinson, a Cornish man, commander of the *Hopewell*, a stout ship of three hundred tons, came to my house. I had formerly been surgeon of another ship where he was master, and a fourth part owner, in a voyage to the Levant. He had always treated me more like a brother than an inferior officer, and hearing of my arrival made me a visit, as I apprehended only out of friendship, for nothing passed more than what is usual after long absences.

But repeating his visits often, expressing his joy to find me in good health, asking whether I were now settled for life, adding that he intended a voyage to the East Indies in two months; at last he plainly invited me, though with some apologies, to be surgeon of the ship. He told me that I should have another surgeon under me besides our two mates; that my salary should be double the usual pay; and that having experienced my knowledge in sea affairs to be at least equal to his, he would enter into any engagement to follow my advice, as much as if I had share in the command.

He said so many other obliging things, and I knew him to be so honest a man, that I could not reject his proposal. The thirst I had of seeing the world, notwithstanding my past misfortunes, continuing as violent as ever. The only difficulty that remained was to persuade my wife, whose consent I at last obtained by the prospect of advantage she proposed to her children.

We set out the 5th of August, 1706, and arrived at Fort St. George [Madras, India] the 11th of April, 1707. We stayed there three weeks to refresh our crew, many of whom were sick. From there we went to Tonquin [Indo-China], where the captain resolved to continue some time, because many of the goods he intended to buy were not ready, nor could he expect to be dispatched in some months. Therefore, in hopes to defray some of the charges he must be at, he bought a sloop, loaded it with several sorts of goods, wherewith the Tonquinese usually trade to the neighboring islands, and putting fourteen men on board, whereof three were of the country, he appointed me master of the sloop, and gave me power to traffic for two months, while he transacted his affairs at Tonquin.

We had not sailed more than three days when a great storm arose and we were driven five days to the north-northeast, and then to the east; after which we had fair weather, but still with a pretty strong gale from the west. Upon the tenth day we were chased by two pirates, who soon overtook us, for my sloop was so deep loaden that she sailed very slowly. Neither were we in a condition to defend ourselves.

We were boarded about the same time by both the pirates, who entered furiously at the head of their

196 LAPUTA AND THE HOUYHNHNMS

men, but finding us all prostrate upon our faces (for so I gave order) they pinioned us with strong ropes, and setting a guard upon us, went to search the sloop.

I observed among them a Dutchman, who seemed to be of some authority, though he was not commander of either ship. He knew us by our countenances to be Englishmen, and jabbering to us in his own language swore we should be tied back to back, and thrown into the sea. I spoke Dutch tolerably well. I told him who we were, and begged him in consideration of our being Christians and Protestants, of neighboring countries in strict alliance, that he would move the captains to take some pity on us. This only inflamed his rage. He repeated his threatenings, and turning to his companions, spoke with great vehemence, in the Japanese language, as I suppose, often using the word *Christianos*.

The largest of the two pirate ships was commanded by a Japanese captain, who spoke a little Dutch, but very imperfectly. He came up to me and after several questions, which I answered in great humility, he said we should not die. I made the captain a very low bow, and then turning to the Dutchman, said I was sorry to find more mercy in a heathen than in a brother Christian. But I had soon reason to repent those foolish words; for that malicious reprobate, having often endeavored in vain to persuade both the captains that I might be thrown into the sea (which they would not yield to after the promise made me, that I should not die), prevailed so far as to have a punishment inflicted on me, worse in all human appearance than death itself.

My men were sent by an equal division into both the pirate ships and my sloop new manned. As to myself, it was determined that I should be set adrift in a small canoe, with paddles and a sail, and four days' provisions, which last the Japanese captain was so kind to double out of his own stores, and would permit no man to search me. I got down into the canoe, while the Dutchman, standing upon the deck, loaded me with all the curses and injurious terms his language could afford.

When I was at some distance from the pirates, I discovered by my pocket glass several islands to the southeast. I set up my sail, the wind being fair, with a design to reach the nearest of those islands, which I made a shift to do in about three hours. It was all rocky. However, I got many birds' eggs, and striking fire, I kindled some heath and dry seaweed, by which I roasted my eggs. I ate no other supper, being resolved to spare my provisions as much as I could. I passed the night under the shelter of a rock, strewing some heath under me, and slept pretty well.

The next day I sailed to another island, and then to a third and fourth, sometimes using my sail and sometimes my paddles. But not to trouble the reader

with a particular account of my distresses, let it suffice that on the fifth day I arrived at the last island in my sight, which lay south-southeast to the former.

This island was at a greater distance than I expected and I did not reach it in less than five hours. I encompassed it almost around before I could find a convenient place to land in, which was a small creek about three times the wideness of my canoe.

I found the island to be all rocky, only a little intermingled with tufts of grass and sweet-smelling herbs. I took out my small provisions, and after having refreshed myself, I secured the remainder in a cave, whereof there were great numbers. I gathered plenty of eggs upon the rocks, and got a quantity of dry seaweed and parched grass, which I designed to kindle the next day, and roast my eggs as well as I could. (For I had about me my flint, steel, match, and burning glass.) I lay all night in the cave where I had lodged my provisions. My bed was the same dry grass and seaweed which I intended for fuel.

I slept very little, for the disquiets of my mind prevailed over my weariness, and kept me awake. I considered how impossible it was to preserve my life in so desolate a place and how miserable my end must be. Yet I found myself so listless and desponding that I had not the heart to rise, and before I could get spirits enough to creep out of my cave the day was far advanced.

I walked awhile among the rocks. The sky was perfectly clear, and the sun so hot that I was forced to turn my face from it. Then all of a sudden it became obscured, as I thought, in a manner very different from what happens by the interposition of a cloud. I turned back, and perceived a vast opaque body between me and the sun, moving forward toward the island: it seemed to be about two miles high, and hid the sun six or seven minutes, but I did not observe the air to be much colder or the sky more darkened than if I had stood under the shade of a mountain. As it approached nearer over the place where I was it appeared to be a firm substance, the bottom flat, smooth, and shining very bright from the reflection of the sea below.

I stood upon a height about two hundred yards from the shore, and saw this vast body descending almost to a parallel with me, at less than an English mile distance. I took out my pocket perspective, and could plainly discover numbers of people moving up and down the sides of it, which appeared to be sloping, but what those people were doing I was not able to distinguish.

The natural love of life gave me some inward motions of joy, and I was ready to entertain a hope that this adventure might some way or other help to deliver me from the desolate place and condition I was in. But at the same time the reader can hardly

conceive my astonishment, to behold an island in the
air, inhabited by men, who were able (as it would
seem) to raise or sink, or put it into a progressive
motion, as they pleased.

But not being at that time in a disposition to phi-
losophize upon this phenomenon, I rather chose to
observe what course the island would take, because
it seemed for a while to stand still. Yet soon after it
advanced nearer, and I could see the sides of it, encompassed with several gradations of galleries, and
stairs at certain intervals, to descend from one to the
other. In the lowest gallery I beheld some people
fishing with long angling rods, and others looking on.

I waved my cap (for my hat was long since worn
out) and my handkerchief toward the island. And
upon its nearer approach, I called and shouted with
the utmost strength of my voice; and then looking
circumspectly, I beheld a crowd gather to that side
which was most in my view. I found by their pointing toward me and to each other that they plainly
discovered me, although they made no return to my
shouting. But I could see four or five men running
in great haste up the stairs to the top of the island
and then disappear. I happened rightly to conjecture that these were sent for orders to some person
in authority upon this occasion.

The number of people increased, and in less than
half an hour the island was moved and raised in such

a manner that the lowest gallery appeared in a parallel of less than a hundred yards distance from the height where I stood. I then put myself into the most supplicating postures, and spoke in the humblest accent but received no answer. Those who stood nearest over against me seemed to be persons of distinction, as I supposed by their habit. They conferred earnestly with each other, looking often upon me. At length one of them called out in a clear, polite, smooth dialect, not unlike in sound to the Italian. Therefore I returned an answer in that language, hoping at least that the cadence might be more agreeable to his ears. Although neither of us understood the other, yet my meaning was easily known, for the people saw the distress I was in.

They made signs for me to come down from the rock and go toward the shore, which I accordingly did. The flying island being raised to a convenient height, the verge directly over me, a chain was let down from the lowest gallery, with a seat fastened to the bottom, to which I fixed myself and was drawn up by pulleys.

CHAPTER 16

Laputa and Its People

A T MY ALIGHTING I was surrounded by a crowd of people, but those who stood nearest seemed to be of better quality. They beheld me with all the marks and circumstances of wonder. Neither indeed was I much in their debt, having never till then seen a race of mortals so singular in their shapes, habits, and countenances. Their heads were all reclined either to the right or the left; one of their eyes turned inward, and the other directly up to the zenith. Their outward garments were adorned with the figures of suns, moons, and stars, interwoven with those of fiddles, flutes, harps, trumpets, guitars, harpsichords, and many other instruments of music unknown to us in Europe.

I observed here and there many in the habit of servants, with a blown bladder fastened like a flail to the end of a short stick, which they carried in their hands. In each bladder was a small quantity of dried peas, or little pebbles (as I was afterward informed). With these bladders they now and then flapped the mouths and ears of those who stood near them, of which practice I could not then conceive the meaning.

It seems the minds of these people are so taken up with intense speculations that they neither can speak nor attend to the discourses of others without being roused by some external taction upon the organs of speech and hearing; for which reason those persons who are able to afford it always keep a flapper in their family, as one of their domestics, nor ever walk abroad or make visits without him. And the business of this officer is, when two or more persons are in company, gently to strike with his bladder the mouth of him who is to speak, and the right ear of him or them to whom the speaker addresses himself. This flapper is likewise employed diligently to attend his master in his walks, and upon occasion to give him a soft flap on his eyes, because he is always so wrapped up in cogitation that he is in manifest danger of falling down every precipice, and bouncing his head against every post, and in the streets, of jostling others, or being jostled himself into the kennel.

It was necessary to give the reader this informa-

tion, without which he would be at the same loss
with me to understand the proceedings of these people, as they conducted me up the stairs, to the top of
the island, and from there to the royal palace. While
we were ascending, they forgot several times what
they were about, and left me to myself, till their
memories were again roused by their flappers. For
they appeared altogether unmoved by the sight of
my foreign habit and countenance, and by the shouts
of the vulgar, whose thoughts and minds were more
disengaged.

At last we entered the palace, and proceeded into
the chamber of presence, where I saw the King
seated on his throne, attended on each side by persons of prime quality. Before the throne was a large
table filled with globes and spheres, and mathematical instruments of all kinds. His Majesty took not the
least notice of us, although our entrance was not
without sufficient noise, by the concourse of all persons belonging to the court. But he was then deep
in a problem, and we attended at least an hour before he could solve it.

There stood by him on each side a young page,
with flaps in their hands, and when they saw he was
at leisure one of them gently struck his mouth, and
the other his right ear. Thereupon he started like one
awakened on the sudden, and looking toward me
and the company I was in, recollected the occasion

Conceive my astonishment to behold an island in the air

[SEE PAGE 207]

of our coming, whereof he had been informed before. He spoke some words, whereupon immediately a young man with a flap came up to my side, and flapped me gently on the right ear. But I made signs, as well as I could, that I had no occasion for such an instrument; which, as I afterward found, gave his Majesty and the whole court a very mean opinion of my understanding.

The King, as far as I could conjecture, asked me several questions, and I addressed myself to him in all the languages I had. When it was found that I could neither understand nor be understood, I was conducted by the King's order to an apartment in his palace where two servants were appointed to attend me.

My dinner was brought, and four persons of quality, whom I remembered to have seen very near the King's person, did me the honor to dine with me. We had two courses of three dishes each. In the first course there was a shoulder of mutton, cut into an equilateral triangle, a piece of beef into a rhomboid, and a pudding into a cycloid. The second course was two ducks, trussed up into the form of fiddles; sausages and puddings resembling flutes and hautboys, and a breast of veal in the shape of a harp. The servants cut our bread into cones, cylinders, parallelograms, and several other mathematical figures.

While we were at dinner I made bold to ask the names of several things in their language. And those noble persons, by the assistance of their flappers, delighted to give me answers, hoping to raise my admiration of their great abilities, if I could be brought to converse with them. I was soon able to call for bread and drink, or whatever else I wanted.

After dinner my company withdrew, and a person was sent to me by the King's order, attended by a flapper. He brought with him pen, ink, and paper, and three or four books, giving me to understand by signs that he was sent to teach me the language. We sat together four hours, in which time I wrote down a great number of words in columns, with the translations over against them. I likewise made a shift to learn several short sentences. For my tutor would order one of my servants to fetch something, to turn about, to make a bow, to sit, or stand, or walk, and the like. Then I took down the sentence in writing.

He showed me also in one of his books the figures of the sun, moon, and stars, the zodiac, the tropics, and polar circles, together with the denominations of many figures of planes and solids. He gave me the names and descriptions of all the musical instruments, and the general terms of art in playing on each of them. After he had left me, I placed all my words with their interpretations in alphabetical order. And thus in a few days, by the help of a very

faithful memory, I got some insight into their language.

Those to whom the King had entrusted me, observing how ill I was clad, ordered a tailor to come next morning and take my measure for a suit of clothes. This operator did his office after a different manner from those of his trade in Europe. He first took my height by a quadrant, and then with a rule and compasses described the dimensions and outlines of my whole body, all which he entered upon paper, and in six days brought my clothes very ill made, and quite out of shape, by happening to mistake a figure in the calculation. But my comfort was that I observed such accidents very frequent, and little regarded.

During my confinement for want of clothes, and by an indisposition that held me some days longer, I much enlarged my dictionary. When I went next to court I was able to understand many things the King spoke, and to return him some kind of answers. His Majesty had given orders that the island should move northeast and by east, to the vertical point over Lagado, the metropolis of the whole kingdom below upon the firm earth. It was about ninety leagues distant, and our voyage lasted four days and an half. I was not in the least sensible of the progressive motion made in the air by the island.

On the second morning about eleven o'clock, the King himself in person, attended by his nobility, courtiers, and officers, having prepared all their musical instruments, played on them for three hours without intermission, so that I was quite stunned with the noise. Neither could I possibly guess the meaning, till my tutor informed me. He said that the people of their island had their ears adapted to hear the music of the spheres, which always played at certain periods, and the court was now prepared to bear their part in whatever instrument they most excelled.

In our journey toward Lagado, the capital city, his Majesty ordered that the island should stop over certain towns and villages, from whence he might receive the petitions of his subjects. And to this purpose several packthreads were let down with small weights at the bottom. On these packthreads the people strung their petitions, which mounted up directly like the scraps of paper fastened by schoolboys at the end of the string that holds their kite. Sometimes we received wine and victuals from below, which were drawn up by pulleys.

The knowledge I had in mathematics gave me great assistance in acquiring their phraseology, which depended much upon that science and music; and in the latter I was not unskilled. Their ideas are perpetually conversant in lines and figures. If they would, for example, praise the beauty of a woman, or any other animal, they describe it by rhombs, circles, parallelograms, ellipses, and other geometrical terms, or by words of art drawn from music. I observed in the King's kitchen all sorts of mathematical and musical instruments, after the figures of which they cut up the joints that were served to his Majesty's table.

Their houses are very ill built, the walls bevel without one right angle in any apartment. This defect arises from the contempt they bear to practical geometry, which they despise as vulgar and me-

chanic, those instructions they give being too refined for the minds of their workmen, which occasions perpetual mistakes. And although they are dexterous enough upon a piece of paper in the management of the rule, the pencil, and the divider, yet in the common actions and behavior of life, I have not seen a more clumsy, awkward, and unhandy people, nor so slow and perplexed in their conceptions upon all other subjects except those of mathematics and music. They are very bad reasoners, and vehemently given to opposition, unless when they happen to be of the right opinion, which is seldom their case. Imagination, fancy, and invention, they are wholly strangers to, nor have any words in their language by which those ideas can be expressed.

These people are under continual disquietudes, never enjoying a minute's peace of mind. Their apprehensions arise from several changes they dread in the celestial bodies. For instance, they fear that the earth, by the continual approaches of the sun toward it, must in course of time be absorbed or swallowed up; and that the earth very narrowly escaped a brush from the tail of the last comet, which would have reduced it to ashes; and that the next, which they have calculated for thirty-one years hence, will probably destroy us. They believe the sun, by daily spending its rays without any fresh nutriment to supply them, will at last be wholly consumed and annihilated.

They are so alarmed with the apprehensions of these and the like impending dangers that they can neither sleep quietly in their beds nor have any relish for the common pleasures or amusements of life. When they meet an acquaintance in the morning, the first question is about the sun's health, how he looked at his setting and rising, and what hopes they have to avoid the stroke of the approaching comet. This conversation they are apt to run into with the same temper that boys show in listening to terrible stories of sprites and hobgoblins and then dare not go to bed for fear.

The wives and daughters lament their confinement to the island, although I think it the most delicious spot of ground in the world. Although they live here in the greatest plenty and magnificence, and

are allowed to do whatever they please, they long to
see the world, and take the diversions of the metropolis, which they are not allowed to do without a particular license from the King. This is not easy to be
obtained, because the people of quality have found
by frequent experience how hard it is to persuade
their women to return from below.

In about a month's time I had learned their language fairly well and was able to answer most of the
King's questions, when I had the honor to attend
him. His Majesty showed not the least curiosity
about the laws, government, history, religion, or
manners of the countries where I had been, but confined his questions to the state of mathematics, and
received the account I gave him with great contempt and indifference, though often roused by his
flapper on each side.

The King graciously allowed me to look about the
island, attended by my tutor. I chiefly wanted to
know to what cause in art or in nature it owed its
several motions.

The Flying, or Floating, Island is exactly circular,
about four and a half miles in diameter, and consequently contains ten thousand acres. It is three hundred yards thick. The under surface, which appears
to those who view it from below, is one even regular
plate of adamant,[1] shooting up to the height of about
two hundred yards. Above it lie the several minerals

[1] An imaginary stone so hard as to be impenetrable.

in their usual order, and over all is a coat of rich mold, ten or twelve feet deep. The slope of the upper surface, from the circumference to the center, causes all the dews and rains to be conveyed in small rivulets toward the middle, where they are emptied into four large basins, each of about half a mile in circuit and two hundred yards distant from the center. From these basins the water is continually exhaled by the sun in the daytime, which prevents their overflowing. Besides, as it is in the power of the monarch to raise the island above the region of clouds and vapors, he can prevent the falling of dews and rains whenever he pleases.

At the center of the island there is a chasm about fifty yards in diameter, from whence the astronomers descend into a large dome, called the astronomer's cave, situated at the depth of a hundred yards beneath the upper surface of the adamant. In this cave twenty lamps are continually burning, thus casting a strong light into every part. The place is stored with great variety of sextants, telescopes, and other astronomical instruments.

But the greatest curiosity, upon which the fate of the island depends, is a loadstone of a prodigious size, in shape resembling a weaver's shuttle. It is in length six yards, and in the thickest part at least three yards over. This magnet is sustained by a very strong axle of adamant passing through its middle,

upon which it plays, and is poised so exactly that the weakest hand can turn it.

By means of this loadstone, the island is made to rise and fall, and move from one place to another. One side of the stone is endowed with an attracting power, and the other with a repelling. Upon placing the magnet erect with its attracting end toward the earth, the island descends; but when the repelling extremity points downward, the island mounts directly upward. When the position of the stone is oblique, the motion of the island is so too. By this oblique motion the island is conveyed to different parts of the monarch's dominions. But it must be observed that this island cannot move beyond the extent of the dominions below, nor can it rise above the height of four miles.

When the stone is put parallel to the plane of the horizon, the island stands still; for in that case the extremities of it being at equal distance from the earth, act with equal force, the one in drawing downward, the other in pushing upward, and consequently no motion can ensue.

If any town should engage in rebellion, fall into violent factions, or refuse to pay the usual tribute, the King has two methods of reducing them to obedience. The first and the mildest course is by keeping the island hovering over such a town, and the lands about it, whereby he can deprive them of the benefit of the sun and the rain, and consequently afflict the inhabitants with dearth and diseases. And if the crime deserve it, they are at the same time pelted from above with great stones, against which they have no defense but by creeping into cellars or caves, while the roofs of their houses are beaten to pieces. But if they still continue obstinate or offer to raise insurrections, he proceeds to the last remedy: by letting the island drop directly upon their heads, which makes a universal destruction both of houses and men. However, this is an extremity to which the prince is seldom driven, neither indeed is he willing to put it in execution.

But there is still a more weighty reason why the kings of this country have always avoided so terrible an action. For if the town intended to be destroyed should have in it any tall rocks or high spires of stone, a sudden fall might endanger the bottom or under surface of the island. Although it consist, as I have said, of one entire adamant two hundred yards thick, it might happen to crack by too great a shock, or burst by approaching too near the fires from the houses below, as the backs both of iron and stone will often do in our chimneys. Of all this the people are well apprised, and understand how far to carry their obstinacy, where their liberty or property is concerned.

CHAPTER 17

The Grand Academy

at Lagado

LTHOUGH I CANNOT SAY that I was ill treated in this island, yet I must confess I thought myself too much neglected. For neither prince nor people appeared to be curious in any part of knowledge, except mathematics and music, wherein I was far their inferior, and upon that account very little regarded.

On the other side, after having seen all the curiosities of the island, I was very desirous to leave it, being heartily weary of those people. They were indeed excellent in two sciences for which I have great esteem, and wherein I am not unversed. But at the same time they are so abstracted and involved in speculation that I never met with such disagreeable companions. I conversed only with women, tradesmen, flappers, and court pages, during two months of my abode there, by which at last I rendered myself extremely contemptible. Yet these were the only people from whom I could ever receive a reasonable answer.

I had obtained by hard study a good degree of knowledge in their language. I was weary of being confined to an island where I received so little countenance, and resolved to leave it with the first opportunity.

There was a great lord at court, nearly related to the King, and for that reason alone used with respect. He was universally reckoned the most ignorant and stupid person among them. He had performed many eminent services for the Crown, had great natural and acquired parts, adorned with integrity and honor, but so ill an ear for music that his detractors reported he had been often known to beat time in the wrong place. Neither could his tutors without extreme difficulty teach him to demonstrate the most easy proposition in mathematics. He was pleased to show me many marks of favor, often did me the honor of a visit, desired to be informed in the affairs of Europe, the laws and customs, the manners and learning of the several countries where I had traveled. He listened to me with great attention, and made very wise observations on all I spoke. He had two flappers attending him for state, but never made use of them except at court and in visits of ceremony, and would always command them to withdraw when we were alone together.

I entreated this illustrious person to intercede in

my behalf with his Majesty for leave to depart, which he accordingly did, as he was pleased to tell me, with regret. For, indeed, he had made me several offers very advantageous, which however I refused with expressions of the highest acknowledgment.

On the 16th day of February I took leave of his Majesty and the court. The King made me a present to the value of about two hundred pounds English, and my protector his kinsman as much more, together with a letter of recommendation to a friend of his in Lagado, the metropolis. The island being then hovering over a mountain about two miles from it, I was let down from the lowest gallery, in the same manner as I had been taken up.

The continent, as far as it is subject to the monarch of the Flying Island, passes under the general name of Balnibarbi, and the metropolis, as I said before, is called Lagado. I felt some little satisfaction in finding myself on firm ground. I walked to the city without any concern, being clad like one of the natives, and sufficiently instructed to converse with them. I soon found out the person's house to whom I was recommended, presented my letter from his friend the grandee in the island, and was received with much kindness. This great lord, whose name was Munodi, ordered me an apartment in his own house, where I continued during my stay, and was entertained in a most hospitable manner.

The next morning after my arrival, he took me in his chariot to see the town, which is about half the size of London, but the houses very strangely built, and most of them out of repair. The people in the streets walked fast, looked wild, their eyes fixed, and were generally in rags. We passed through one of the town gates, and went about three miles into the country, where I saw many laborers working with several sorts of tools in the ground, but was not able to conjecture what they were about. Neither did I observe any expectation either of corn or grass, although the soil appeared to be excellent. I could not forbear wondering at these odd appearances both

in town and country, and I made bold to desire my
conductor that he would be pleased to explain to me
what could be meant by so many busy heads, hands,
and faces, both in the streets and the fields, because
I did not discover any good effects they produced;
but on the contrary, I never knew a soil so unhappily
cultivated, houses so ill contrived and so ruinous, or
a people whose countenances and habit expressed
so much misery and want.

When I gave that free censure of the country and
its inhabitants, he made no further answer than by
telling me that I had not been long enough among
them to form a judgment, and that the different nations of the world had different customs, with other
common topics to the same purpose. But when we
returned to his palace, he asked me how I liked the
building, what absurdities I observed, and what
quarrel I had with the dress or looks of his domestics.
This he might safely do, because everything about
him was magnificent, regular, and polite. I answered
that his Excellency's prudence, quality, and fortune
had exempted him from those defects which folly
and beggary had produced in others. He said if I
would go with him to his country house, about
twenty miles distant, where his estate lay, there
would be more leisure for this kind of conversation.
I told his Excellency that I was entirely at his disposal, and accordingly we set out next morning.

During our journey he made me observe the several methods used by farmers in managing their lands, which to me were wholly unaccountable. For except in some very few places I could not discover one ear of corn or blade of grass. But in three hours' traveling the scene was wholly altered. We came into a most beautiful country: farmers' houses at small distances, neatly built; the fields enclosed, containing vineyards, corn grounds, and meadows. Neither do I remember to have seen a more delightful prospect. His Excellency observed my countenance to clear up. He told me with a sigh that there his estate began, and would continue the same till we should come to his house. He said that his countrymen ridiculed and despised him for managing his af-

fairs no better, and for setting so ill an example to the
kingdom, which however was followed by very few,
such as were old, and willful, and weak like himself.

We came at length to the house, which was indeed a noble structure, built according to the best
rules of ancient architecture. The fountains, gardens, walks, avenues, and groves were all disposed
with exact judgment and taste. I gave due praises to
everything I saw, whereof his Excellency took not
the least notice till after supper, when, there being
no third companion, he told me with a very melancholy air that he doubted he must throw down his
houses in town and country, to rebuild them after
the present mode, destroy all his plantations, and
cast others into such a form as modern usage required, and give the same directions to all his ten-
ants, unless he would submit to incur the censure of
pride, singularity, affectation, ignorance, caprice,
and perhaps increase his Majesty's displeasure.

The sum of his discourse was to this effect. That
about forty years ago certain persons went up to Laputa, either upon business or diversion, and after
five months' continuance came back with a very
little smattering in mathematics, but full of volatile
spirits acquired in that airy region. That these persons upon their return began to dislike the management of everything below, and fell into schemes of
putting all arts, sciences, languages, and mechanics

upon a new foot. To this end they procured a royal patent for erecting an Academy of Projectors in Lagado. And the humor prevailed so strongly among the people that there is not a town of any consequence in the kingdom without such an academy.

In these colleges the professors contrive new rules and methods of agriculture and building, and new instruments and tools for all trades and manufactures, whereby, as they undertake, one man shall do the work of ten. A palace may be built in a week, of materials so durable as to last forever without repairing. All the fruits of the earth shall come to maturity at whatever season we think fit to choose, and increase a hundredfold more than they do at present, with innumerable other happy proposals. The only inconvenience is that none of these projects are yet brought to perfection, and in the meantime the whole country lies miserably waste, the houses in ruins, and the people without food or clothes. By all which, instead of being discouraged, they are fifty times more violently bent upon prosecuting their schemes, driven equally on by hope and despair; that as for himself, being not of an enterprising spirit, he was content to go on in the old forms, to live in the houses his ancestors had built, and act as they did in every part of life without innovation. That some few other persons of quality and gentry had done the same, but were looked on with an eye of contempt and ill will, as enemies to art, ignorant, and ill commonwealth's-men, preferring their own ease and sloth before the general improvement of their country.

In a few days we came back to town, and his Excellency, considering the bad character he had in the Academy, would not go with me himself, but recommended me to a friend of his to bear me company thither. My lord was pleased to represent me as a great admirer of projects, and a person of much curiosity and easy belief; which, indeed, was not without truth, for I had myself been a sort of projector in my younger days.

This Academy is not an entire single building, but a continuation of several houses on both sides of a street, which going to waste was purchased and applied to that use.

I was received very kindly by the warden, and went for many days to the Academy. Every room has in it one or more projectors, and I believe I could not have been in fewer than five hundred rooms.

The first man I saw was of a meager aspect, with sooty hands and face, his hair and beard long, ragged, and singed in several places. His clothes, shirt, and skin were all of the same color. He had been eight years upon a project for extracting sunbeams out of cucumbers, which were to be put into vials hermetically sealed, and let out to warm the air in raw inclement summers. He told me he did not doubt in eight years more he should be able to supply the Governor's gardens with sunshine at a reasonable rate. But he complained that his stock was low, and entreated me to give him something as an encouragement to ingenuity, especially since this had been a very dear season for cucumbers. I made him a small present, for my lord had furnished me with money on purpose, because he knew their practice of begging from all who go to see them.

There was a most ingenious architect who had contrived a new method for building houses, by beginning at the roof, and working downward to the foundation, which he justified to me by the like practice of those two prudent insects, the bee and the spider.

There was a man born blind, who had several apprentices in his own condition. Their employment was to mix colors for painters, which their master taught them to distinguish by feeling and smelling. It was indeed my misfortune to find them at that time not very perfect in their lessons, and the professor himself happened to be generally mistaken. This artist is much encouraged and esteemed by the whole fraternity.

I went into another room, where the walls and ceiling were all hung round with cobwebs, except a narrow passage for the artist to go in and out. At my

entrance he called aloud to me not to disturb his webs. He lamented the fatal mistake the world had been so long in of using silkworms, while we had such plenty of domestic insects, who infinitely excelled the former because they understood how to weave as well as spin. And he proposed further that by employing spiders the charge of dyeing silks should be wholly saved, whereof I was fully convinced when he showed me a vast number of flies most beautifully colored, wherewith he fed his spiders, assuring us that the webs would take a tincture from them. And as he had them of all hues, he hoped to fit everybody's fancy, as soon as he could find proper food for the flies, of certain gums, oils, and other glutinous matter to give a strength and consistence to the threads.

I had hitherto seen only one side of the Academy, the other being appropriated to the advancers of speculative learning, of which I shall say something when I have mentioned one illustrious person more, who is called among them *the universal artist*. He told us he had been thirty years employing his thoughts for the improvement of human life. He had two large rooms full of wonderful curiosities, and fifty men at work.

Some were condensing air into a dry tangible substance, by extracting the niter, and letting the aqueous or fluid particles percolate. Others were softening marbles for pillows and pincushions; others petrifying the hoofs of a living horse to preserve them from foundering. The artist himself was at that time busy upon two great designs: the first, to sow land with chaff, wherein he affirmed the true seminal virtue to be contained, as he demonstrated by several experiments which I was not skillful enough to comprehend. The other was, by a certain composition of gums, minerals, and vegetables outwardly applied, to prevent the growth of wool upon two young lambs. He hoped in a reasonable time to propagate the breed of naked sheep all over the kingdom.

We crossed a walk to the other part of the Academy, where, as I have already said, the projectors in speculative learning resided.

The first professor I saw was in a very large room, with forty pupils about him. After salutation, observing me to look earnestly upon a frame which took up the greatest part of both the length and breadth of the room, he said perhaps I might wonder to see him employed in a project for improving speculative knowledge by practical and mechanical operations. But the world would soon be sensible of its usefulness, and he flattered himself that a more noble exalted thought never sprang in any other man's head. Everyone knew how laborious the usual method is of attaining to arts and sciences; whereas by his contrivance the most ignorant person at a reasonable charge, and with a little bodily labor, may write books in philosophy, poetry, politics, law, mathematics, and theology, without the least assistance from genius or study.

He then led me to the frame, about the sides

whereof all his pupils stood in ranks. It was twenty feet square, placed in the middle of the room. The surface was composed of several bits of wood, about the bigness of a die, but some larger than others. They were all linked together by slender wires. These bits of wood were covered on every square with paper pasted on them, and on these papers were written all the words of their language, in their several moods, tenses, and declensions, but without any order.

The professor then desired me to observe, for he was going to set his engine at work. The pupils at his command took each of them hold of an iron handle, whereof there were forty fixed round the edges of the frame, and giving them a sudden turn, the whole disposition of the words was entirely changed. He then commanded thirty-six of the lads to read the several lines softly as they appeared upon the frame. And where they found three or four words together that might make part of a sentence, they dictated to the four remaining boys, who were scribes. This work was repeated three or four times, and at every turn the engine was so contrived that the words shifted into new places, as the square bits of wood moved upside down.

Six hours a day the young students were employed in this labor, and the professor showed me several volumes in large folio already collected, of broken

sentences which he intended to piece together, and out of those rich materials to give the world a complete body of all arts and sciences.

We next went to the school of languages, where three professors sat in consultation upon improving that of their own country.

The first project was to shorten discourse by cutting polysyllables into one, and leaving out verbs and participles, because in reality all things imaginable are but nouns.

The other project was a scheme for entirely abolishing all words whatsoever. This was urged as a great advantage in point of health as well as brevity. For it is plain that every word we speak is in some degree a diminution of our lungs by corrosion, and consequently contributes to the shortening of our lives. An expedient was therefore offered: since words are only names for *things,* it would be more convenient for all men to carry about them such things as were necessary to express the particular business they are to discourse on.

And this invention would certainly have taken place, to the great ease as well as health of the subject, if the women, in conjunction with the vulgar and illiterate, had not threatened to raise a rebellion, unless they might be allowed the liberty to speak with their tongues, after the manner of their ancestors. Such constant irreconcilable enemies to science are the common people. However, many of the most learned and wise adhere to the new scheme of expressing themselves by things, which has only this inconvenience attending it, that if a man's business be very great, and of various kinds, he must be obliged in proportion to carry a greater bundle of things upon his back, unless he can afford one or two strong servants to attend him.

I have often beheld two of those sages almost sinking under the weight of their packs, like peddlers among us; who, when they met in the streets, would lay down their loads, open their sacks, and hold conversation for an hour together; then put up their implements, help each other to resume their burdens, and take their leave.

But for short conversations a man may carry implements in his pockets and under his arms, enough to supply him, and in his house he cannot be at a loss. Therefore the room where company meet who practice this art is full of all things ready at hand requisite to furnish matter for this kind of artificial converse.

I was at the mathematical school, where the master taught his pupils after a method scarce imaginable to us in Europe. The proposition and demonstration was fairly written on a thin wafer, with a special kind of ink. This the student was to swallow upon a fasting stomach, and for three days following eat nothing but bread and water. As the wafer digested, the ink mounted to his brain bearing the proposition along with it. But the success has not hitherto been answerable, partly by some error in the composition of the ink and partly by the perverseness of lads, to whom this pill is so nauseous that they generally steal aside and only pretend to swallow it; also they have not yet been persuaded to use so long an abstinence as the prescription requires.

I saw nothing in this country that could invite me to a longer continuance, and began to think of returning home to England.

CHAPTER 18

The Land of Magic—

Japan—Then Home

THE CONTINENT of which this kingdom is a part extends itself, as I have reason to believe, eastward to that unknown tract of America, westward to California, and north to the Pacific Ocean, which is not above a hundred and fifty miles from Lagado, where there is a good port and much commerce with the great island of Luggnagg. The island of Luggnagg stands southeastward of Japan, about a hundred leagues distant. There is a strict alliance between the Japanese Emperor and the King of Luggnagg, which affords frequent opportunities of sailing from one island to the other.

I determined therefore to direct my course this way, in order to return to Europe. I hired two mules with a guide to show me the way, and carry my small baggage. I took leave of my noble protector, who

We entered the gate between two rows of guards

had shown me so much favor and made me a generous present at my departure.

When I arrived at the port of Maldonada there
was no ship in the harbor bound for Luggnagg, nor
likely to be in some time. I soon fell into some acquaintance, and was very hospitably received. A
gentleman of distinction said to me that since the
ship bound for Luggnagg could not be ready in less
than a month, it might be no disagreeable amuse-
ment for me to take a trip to the little island of
Glubbdubdrib, about five leagues off to the southwest. He offered himself and a friend to accompany

me, and that I should be provided with a small convenient barque for the voyage.

Glubbdubdrib, as nearly as I can interpret the word, signifies the Island of Sorcerers or Magicians. It is about one-third as large as the Isle of Wight, and extremely fruitful. It is governed by the head of a certain tribe, who are all magicians. The eldest in succession is prince or governor. He has a noble palace, and a park of about three thousand acres, surrounded by a wall of hewn stone twenty feet high. In this park are several small enclosures for cattle, corn, and gardening.

The Governor and his family are served and attended by domestics of a kind somewhat unusual. By his skill in necromancy he has a power of calling whom he pleases from the dead and commanding their service for twenty-four hours, but no longer. Nor can he call the same persons up again in less than three months, except upon very extraordinary occasions.

When we arrived at the island, which was about eleven in the morning, one of the gentlemen who accompanied me went to the Governor and desired admittance for a stranger, who came on purpose to have the honor of attending on his Highness. This was immediately granted, and we all three entered the gate of the palace between two rows of guards, armed and dressed after a very antique manner, and something in their countenances made my flesh creep with a horror I cannot express. We passed through several apartments, between servants of the same sort, ranked on each side as before, till we came to the chamber of presence, where, after three profound obeisances and a few general questions, we were permitted to sit on three stools near the lowest step of his Highness's throne. He understood the language of Balnibarbi, although it was different from that of his island. He desired me to give him some account of my travels; and to let me see that I should be treated without ceremony he dismissed all his attendants with a turn of his finger, at which to my great astonishment they vanished in an instant, like visions in a dream when we awake on a sudden. I could not recover myself in some time, till the Governor assured me that I should receive no hurt.

Observing my two companions to be under no concern, who had been often entertained in the same manner, I began to take courage and related to his Highness a short history of my several adventures, yet not without some hesitation, and frequently looking behind me to the place where I had seen those domestic specters. I had the honor to dine with the Governor, where a new set of ghosts served up the meat and waited at table. I now observed myself to be less terrified than I had been in the morning. I stayed till sunset, but humbly desired his Highness to excuse me for not accepting his invitation of lodging in the palace. My two friends and I lay at a private house in the town adjoining, which is the capital of this little island; and the next morning we returned to pay our duty to the Governor, as he was pleased to command us.

After this manner we continued in the island for ten days, most part of every day with the Governor and at night in our lodging. I soon grew so familiarized to the sight of spirits that the third or fourth time they gave me no emotion at all, or, if I had any apprehensions left, my curiosity prevailed over them. For his Highness the Governor ordered me to call up whatever persons I would choose to name, and in whatever numbers among all the dead from the beginning of the world to the present time, and command them to answer any questions I should think fit to ask; with this condition, that my questions must be confined within the compass of the times they lived in. And one thing I might depend upon, they would certainly tell me truth, for lying was a talent of no use in the lower world.

I made my humble acknowledgments to his Highness for so great a favor. We were in a chamber from whence there was a fair prospect into the park. And because my first inclination was to be entertained with scenes of pomp and magnificence, I desired to see Alexander the Great, at the head of his army just after the battle of Arbela. Upon a motion of the Governor's finger he immediately appeared in a large field under the window where we stood. Alexander was called up into the room. It was with great difficulty that I understood his Greek, and had but little of my own. He assured me upon his honor that he was not poisoned, but died of a fever by excessive drinking.

Next I saw Hannibal passing the Alps, who told me he had not a drop of vinegar in his camp.

I saw Caesar and Pompey at the head of their troops, just ready to engage. I saw the former in his last great triumph. I desired that the senate of Rome might appear before me in one large chamber, and an assembly of somewhat a later age in counterview in another. The first seemed to be an assembly of heroes and demigods; the other a knot of peddlers, pickpockets, highwaymen, and bullies.

The Governor at my request gave the sign for Caesar and Brutus to advance toward us. I was struck with a profound veneration at the sight of Brutus, and could easily discover the most consummate virtue, the greatest intrepidity and firmness of mind, the truest love of his country, and general benevolence for mankind in every lineament of his countenance. I observed with much pleasure that these two persons were in good intelligence with each other, and Caesar freely confessed to me that the greatest actions of his own life were not equal by many degrees to the glory of taking it away. I had the honor to have much conversation with Brutus; and was told that his ancestor Junius, Socrates, Epaminondas, Cato the younger, Sir Thomas More, and himself were perpetually together: a sextumvirate to which all the ages of the world cannot add a seventh.

I had a deep desire to see the world in every period of antiquity. I chiefly fed my eyes with beholding the destroyers of tyrants and usurpers, and the restorers of liberty to oppressed and injured nations. But I particularly wanted to see those ancients who were most renowned for wit and learning. I set apart one day for that purpose. I proposed that Homer and Aristotle might appear at the head of all their commentators. But these were so numerous that some hundreds were forced to attend in the court and outward rooms of the palace. I knew and could distinguish those two heroes at first sight, not only from the crowd but from each other. Homer was the taller and comelier person of the two, walked very erect for one of his age, and his eyes were the most quick and piercing I ever beheld. Aristotle stooped much, and made use of a staff. His visage was meager, his hair lank and thin, and his voice hollow.

The two gentlemen who conducted me to the island were pressed by their private affairs to return

in three days, which I employed in seeing some of the modern dead, who had made the greatest figure for two or three hundred years past in our own and other countries of Europe. Having been always a great admirer of old illustrious families, I desired the Governor would call up a dozen or two of kings with their ancestors in order for eight or nine generations. But my disappointment was grievous and unexpected. For instead of a long train with royal diadems, I saw in one family two fiddlers, three spruce courtiers, and an Italian prelate; in another, a barber, an abbot, and two cardinals. I have too great a veneration for crowned heads to dwell any longer on so nice a subject. But as to counts, marquesses, dukes, earls, and the like, I was not so scrupulous. And I confess it was not without some pleasure that I found myself able to trace the particular features, by which certain families are distinguished, up to their originals. I could plainly discover from whence one family derives a long chin, why a second has abounded with knaves for two generations, and fools for two more; why a third happened to be crack-brained, and a fourth to be sharpers. How cruelty, falsehood, and cowardice grew to be characteristics by which certain families are distinguished as much as by their coat of arms.

I was chiefly disgusted with modern history. For having strictly examined all the persons of greatest name in the courts of princes for a hundred years past, I found how the world had been misled by writers, to ascribe the greatest exploits in war to cowards, the wisest counsel to fools, Roman virtue to betrayers of their country, piety to atheists, truth to informers; how many innocent and excellent persons had been condemned to death or banishment; how many villains had been exalted to high places.

I took leave of his Highness the Governor of Glubbdubdrib, and returned with my two companions to Maldonada, where after a fortnight's waiting, a ship was ready to sail for Luggnagg. I was a month in this voyage. We had one violent storm, and were under a necessity of steering westward to get into the trade wind. On the 21st of April, 1709, we sailed into the river of Clumegnig, which is a seaport town, at the southeast point of Luggnagg. We cast anchor within a league of the town, and made a signal for a pilot. Two of them came on board in less than half an hour, by whom we were guided between certain shoals and rocks, which are very dangerous in the passage, to a large basin, where a fleet may ride in safety within a cable's length of the town wall.

Some of our sailors, whether out of treachery or inadvertence, had informed the pilots that I was a stranger and a great traveler, whereof these gave notice to a customhouse officer, by whom I was examined very strictly upon my landing. This officer spoke to me in the language of Balnibarbi, which by the force of much commerce is generally understood in that town, especially by seamen and those employed in the customs. I gave him a short account of some particulars, and made my story as plausible and consistent as I could. But I thought it necessary to disguise my country, and call myself an Hollander, because my intentions were for Japan and I knew the Dutch were the only Europeans permitted to enter into that kingdom.

I therefore told the officer that, having been shipwrecked on the coast of Balnibarbi, and cast on a rock, I was received up into Laputa, or the Flying Island (of which he had often heard), and was now endeavoring to get to Japan, from whence I might find a convenience of returning to my own country. The officer said I must be confined till he could receive orders from court, for which he would write immediately, and hoped to receive an answer in a fortnight.

I was carried to a convenient lodging, with a sentry placed at the door. However I had the liberty of a large garden, and was treated with humanity enough, being maintained all the time at the King's charge. I was visited by several persons, chiefly out of curiosity, because it was reported that I came from countries very remote of which they had never heard.

I hired a young man who came in the same ship to be an interpreter. He was a native of Luggnagg, but had lived some years at Maldonada, and was a perfect master of both languages. By his assistance I was able to hold a conversation with those who came to visit me; but this consisted only of their questions and my answers.

The dispatch came from court about the time we expected. It contained a warrant for conducting me and my retinue to Traldragdubb by a party of ten horse. All my retinue was that poor lad for an interpreter, whom I persuaded into my service, and at my humble request we had each of us a mule to ride on. A messenger was dispatched half a day's journey before us, to give the King notice of my approach, and to desire that his Majesty would please appoint a day and hour when it would be his gracious pleasure that I might have the honor to *lick the dust before his footstool.*

This is the court style, and I found it to be more than matter of form. For upon my admittance two days after my arrival, I was commanded to crawl on my belly and lick the floor as I advanced. But on account of my being a stranger, care was taken to have it made so clean that the dust was not offensive. However, this was a peculiar grace, not allowed to any but persons of the highest rank, when they desire an admittance. Nay, sometimes the floor is strewn with dust on purpose, when the person to be admitted happens to have powerful enemies at court. And I have seen a great lord with his mouth so crammed that when he had crept to the proper distance from the throne he was not able to speak a word. Neither is there any remedy, because it is capital for those who receive an audience to spit or wipe their mouths in his Majesty's presence.

There is indeed another custom, which I cannot altogether approve of. When the King has a mind to put any of his nobles to death in a gentle indulgent manner, he commands to have the floor strewn with a certain brown powder, of a deadly composition, which being licked up kills him in twenty-four hours. But in justice to this prince's great clemency, and the care he has of his subjects' lives, it must be mentioned for his honor that strict orders are given to have the infected parts of the floor well washed after every such execution; which if his domestics neglect, they are in danger of incurring his royal displeasure.

When I had crept within four yards of the throne I raised myself gently upon my knees, and then striking my forehead seven times on the ground I pronounced the following words, as they had been taught me the night before, *Ickpling gloffthrobb squutserumm blhiop mlashnalt zwin tnodbalkguffh slhiophad gurdlubh asht.* This is the compliment established by the laws of the land for all persons admitted to the King's presence. It may be rendered into English thus: "May your Celestial Majesty outlive the sun, eleven moons and a half."

To this the King returned some answer, which I could not understand, yet I replied as I had been directed: *Fluft drin yalerick dwuldom prastrad mirpush,* which properly signifies, "My tongue is in the mouth of my friend," and by this expression was meant that I desired leave to bring my interpreter; whereupon the young man already mentioned was accordingly introduced, by whose intervention I answered as many questions as his Majesty could put in over an hour. I spoke in the Balnibarbian tongue, and my interpreter delivered my meaning in that of Luggnagg.

The King was much delighted with my company and ordered his High Chamberlain to appoint a lodging in the court for me and my interpreter, with a daily allowance for my table and a large purse of gold for my common expenses.

I stayed three months in this country out of perfect obedience to his Majesty, who was pleased highly to favor me and made me very honorable offers. But I thought it more consistent with prudence

and justice to pass the remainder of my days with my wife and family.

His Majesty having often pressed me to accept some employment in his court, and finding me absolutely determined to return to my native country, was pleased to give me his license to depart, and honored me with a letter of recommendation under his own hand to the Emperor of Japan.

On the 6th of May, 1709, I took a solemn leave of his Majesty and all my friends. In six days I found a vessel ready to carry me to Japan, and spent fifteen days in the voyage.

We landed at a small port town called Xamoschi, situated on the southeast part of Japan. The town lies on the western point, where there is a narrow strait, leading northward into a long arm of the sea, upon the northwest part of which Yedo the metropolis stands. At landing, I showed the customhouse officers my letter from the King of Luggnagg to his Imperial Majesty.

The magistrates of the town, hearing of my letter, received me as a public minister. They provided me with carriages and servants, and bore my charges to Yedo. Here I was admitted to an audience, and delivered my letter, which was opened with great ceremony, and explained to the Emperor by an interpreter, who then gave me notice by his Majesty's order. This interpreter was a person employed to transact affairs with the Hollanders. He soon conjectured by my countenance that I was a European, and therefore repeated his Majesty's commands in Low Dutch, which he spoke perfectly well. I answered (as I had before determined) that I was a Dutch merchant, shipwrecked in a very remote country, from whence I traveled by sea and land to Luggnagg, and then took shipping for Japan, where I knew my countrymen often traded, and with some of these I hoped to get an opportunity of returning into Europe. I therefore most humbly entreated his royal favor, to give order that I should be conducted in safety to Nangasac.

I arrived at Nangasac, after a very long and troublesome journey. I soon fell into the company of some Dutch sailors belonging to the *Amboyna*, of Amsterdam. I had lived long in Holland, pursuing my studies at Leyden, and I spoke Dutch well. The seamen soon knew from whence I came last. They were curious to inquire into my voyages and course of life. I made up a story as short and probable as I could, but concealed the greatest part. I knew many persons in Holland. I was able to invent names for my parents, whom I pretended to be obscure people in the province of Gelderland. I would have given the captain (one Theodorus Vangrult) what he pleased to ask for my voyage to Holland; but understanding I was a surgeon, he was contented to take half the usual rate, on condition that I would serve him in the way of my calling.

Nothing hap-
pened worth
mentioning in
this voyage. We
sailed with a fair

wind to the Cape of Good Hope, where we stayed
only to take in fresh water. On the 10th of April we
arrived safe at Amsterdam, having lost only three
men by sickness in the voyage, and a fourth who fell
from the foremast into the sea, not far from the coast
of Guinea. From Amsterdam I soon after set sail for
England in a small vessel belonging to that city.

On the 16th of April, 1710, we put in at the Downs.
I landed the next morning, and saw once more my
native country after an absence of five years and six
months complete. I went straight to Redriff, where I
arrived the same day at two in the afternoon, and
found my wife and family in good health.

CHAPTER 19

The Houyhnhnms' Country

ICONTINUED AT HOME with my wife and
children about five months in a very happy
condition, if I could have learned the lesson of
knowing when I was well off. I left my poor
wife and children, and accepted an advantageous
offer made me to be captain of the *Adventure,* a stout
merchantman. We set sail from Portsmouth upon the
7th of August, 1710.

I had several men die in my ship of tropical fever,
so that I was forced to get recruits out of Barbadoes,
and the Leeward Islands, where I touched by the
direction of the merchants who employed me. This
I had soon too much cause to repent, for I found afterward that most of them had been buccaneers. I
had fifty hands on board, and my orders were that I
should trade with the Indians in the South Sea, and
make what discoveries I could. These rogues whom

and the hands of board sh____
as said that, with the ____
casks, which showed ____

I had picked up formed a conspiracy to seize the ship and secure me. This they did one morning, rushing into my cabin, and binding me hand and foot, threatening to throw me overboard if I offered to stir.

I told them I was their prisoner and would submit. This they made me swear to do, and then they unbound me, only fastening one of my legs with a chain near my bed, and placed a sentry at my door with his piece charged, who was commanded to shoot me dead if I attempted my liberty. They sent me down victuals and drink, and took the government of the ship to themselves.

Their design was to turn pirates, and plunder the Spaniards, which they could not do till they got more men. But first they resolved to sell the goods in the ship, and then go to Madagascar for recruits, several among them having died since my confinement. They sailed many weeks, and traded with the Indians, but I knew not what course they took, being kept a close prisoner in my cabin, and expecting nothing less than to be murdered, as they often threatened me.

One day James Welch came down to my cabin and said he had orders from the captain to set me ashore. They forced me into the longboat, letting me put on my best suit of clothes, which were as good as new, and a small bundle of linen, but no arms except my sword. And they were so civil as not to search my pockets, into which I conveyed what money I had, with some other little necessaries. They rowed about a league, and then set me down on a strand. I desired them to tell me what country it was. They all swore they knew no more than myself, but said that the captain was resolved, after they had sold the lading, to get rid of me in the first place where they could discover land. They pushed off immediately, advising me to make haste for fear of being overtaken by the tide, and so bade me farewell.

In this desolate condition I advanced forward, and soon got upon firm ground, where I sat down on a bank to rest myself and consider what I had best do. When I was a little refreshed I went up into the country, resolving to deliver myself to the first savages I should meet, and purchase my life from them by some bracelets, glass rings, and other toys which sailors usually provide themselves with in those voyages.

The land was divided by long rows of trees, not regularly planted, but naturally growing. There was plenty of grass, and several fields of oats. I walked very circumspectly for fear of being surprised, or suddenly shot with an arrow from behind or on either side. I fell into a beaten road, where I saw many tracks of human feet, and some of cows, but most of horses.

At last I beheld several animals in a field, and one

or two of the same kind sitting in trees. Their shape
was very singular and deformed, which a little discomposed me, so that I lay down behind a thicket to
observe them better. Some of them coming forward
near the place where I lay gave me an opportunity
of distinctly marking their form. Their heads and
breasts were covered with a thick hair, some frizzled

and others lank. They had beards like goats, and a long ridge of hair down their backs and the foreparts of their legs and feet, but the rest of their bodies were bare, so that I might see their skins, which were of a brown buff color. Upon the whole, I never beheld in all my travels so disagreeable an animal, nor one against which I naturally conceived so strong an antipathy.

Thinking I had seen enough, full of contempt and aversion, I got up and pursued the beaten road, hoping it might direct me to the cabin of some Indian. I had not got far when I met one of these creatures full in my way, and coming up directly to me. The ugly monster, when he saw me, distorted several ways every feature of his visage, and stared as at an object he had never seen before; then approaching nearer, lifted up his forepaw, whether out of curiosity or mischief, I could not tell. But I drew my sword, and gave him a good blow with the flat side of it, for I dare not strike him with the edge, fearing the inhabitants might be provoked against me, if they should come to know that I had killed or maimed any of their cattle.

When the beast felt the smart, he drew back, and roared so loud that a herd of at least forty came flocking about me from the next field, howling and making odious faces. But I ran to the body of a tree, and leaning my back against it, kept them off by waving my sword.

In the midst of this distress, I observed them all to run away of a sudden as fast as they could, at which I ventured to leave the tree, and pursue the road, wondering what it was that could put them into this fright. But looking on my left hand, I saw a horse walking softly in the field; which my persecutors having sooner discovered, was the cause of their flight.

The horse started a little when he came near me, but soon recovering himself, looked full in my face with manifest tokens of wonder. He viewed my hands and feet, walking round me several times. I would have pursued my journey, but he placed himself directly in the way, yet looking with a very mild aspect, never offering the least violence. We stood gazing at each other for some time. At last I took the boldness to reach my hand toward his neck, with a design to stroke it, using the common style and whistle of jockeys when they are going to handle a strange horse. But this animal, seeming to receive my civilities with disdain, shook his head and bent his brows, softly raising up his right forefoot to remove my hand. Then he neighed three or four times, but in so different a cadence that I almost began to think he was speaking to himself in some language of his own.

While he and I were thus employed, another horse came up; who applying himself to the first in a very formal manner, they gently struck each other's right hoof before, neighing several times by turns, and varying the sound, which seemed to be almost articulate. They went some paces off, as if it were to confer together, walking side by side, backward and forward, like persons deliberating upon some affair of weight, but often turning their eyes toward me, as it were to watch that I might not escape.

I was amazed to see such actions and behavior in brute beasts, and concluded with myself that if the inhabitants of this country were endowed with a proportionable degree of reason they must needs be the wisest people upon earth. This thought gave me so much comfort that I resolved to go forward until I could discover some house or village, or meet with any of the natives, leaving the two horses to discourse together as they pleased. But the first, who was a dapple gray, observing me to steal off, neighed after me in so expressive a tone that I fancied myself to understand what he meant. Whereupon I turned back and came near him, to expect his further commands, but concealing my fear as much as I could, for I began to be in some pain, how this adventure might terminate.

The two horses came up close to me, looking with great earnestness upon my face and hands. The gray steed rubbed my hat all round with his right forehoof, and discomposed it so much that I was forced to adjust it better, by taking it off, and settling it again; whereat both he and his companion (who was

a brown bay) appeared to be much surprised. The latter felt the lappet of my coat, and finding it to hang loose about me, they both looked with new signs of wonder. He stroked my right hand, seeming to admire the softness and color. But he squeezed it so hard between his hoof and his pastern that I was forced to roar; after which they both touched me with all possible tenderness. They were under great perplexity about my shoes and stockings, which they felt very often, neighing to each other, and using various gestures, not unlike those of a philosopher when he would attempt to solve some new and difficult phenomenon.

Upon the whole, the behavior of these animals was so orderly and rational, so acute and judicious, that I at last concluded they must needs be magicians, who had thus metamorphosed themselves upon some design and, seeing a stranger in the way, were resolved to divert themselves with him. Perhaps they were really amazed at the sight of a man so very different in habit, feature, and complexion from those who might probably live in so remote a climate. Upon the strength of this reasoning, I ventured to address them in the following manner:

"Gentlemen, if you be conjurers, as I have good cause to believe, you can understand any language. Therefore I make bold to let your worships know that I am a poor distressed Englishman, driven by his misfortunes upon your coast, and I entreat one of you to let me ride upon his back, as if he were a real horse, to some house or village where I can be relieved. In return of which favor I will make you a present of this knife and bracelet" (taking them out of my pocket).

The two creatures stood silent while I spoke, seeming to listen with great attention. And when I had ended, they neighed frequently toward each other, as if they were engaged in serious conversation. I plainly observed that their language expressed the passions very well, and the words might with little pains be resolved into an alphabet more easily than the Chinese.

I could frequently distinguish the word *Yahoo*, which was repeated by each of them several times. And although it was impossible for me to conjecture what it meant, yet while the two horses were busy in conversation I endeavored to practice this word upon my tongue. And as soon as they were silent, I boldly pronounced Yahoo in a loud voice, imitating, at the same time, as near as I could, the neighing of a horse. At this they were both visibly surprised, and the gray repeated the same word twice, as if he meant to teach me the right accent, wherein I spoke after him as well as I could, and found myself perceivably to improve every time, though very far from any degree of perfection. Then the bay tried me with a second word, much harder to be pronounced; but reducing it to the English orthography, may be spelt thus: *Houyhnhnm*. I did not succeed in this so well as the former, but after two or three further trials, I had better fortune. And they both appeared amazed at my capacity.

After some further discourse, which I then conjectured might relate to me, the two friends took their leave, with the same compliment of striking

each other's hoof. And the gray made me signs that I should walk before him, wherein I thought it prudent to comply, till I could find a better director. When I offered to slacken my pace, he would cry *hhuun, hhuun*. I guessed his meaning, and gave him to understand as well as I could that I was weary, and not able to walk faster; upon which he would stand awhile to let me rest.

Having traveled about three miles, we came to a long kind of building, made of timber stuck in the ground, and wattled across. The roof was low, and covered with straw. I now began to be a little comforted, and took out some toys, which travelers usually carry for presents to the savage Indians of America and other parts, in hopes the people of the house would be thereby encouraged to receive me kindly. The horse made me a sign to go in first.

It was a large room with a smooth clay floor, and a rack and manger extending the whole length on one side. There were three nags, and two mares, not eating, but some of them sitting down upon their hams, which I very much wondered at; but wondered more to see the rest employed in domestic business. These seemed but ordinary cattle; however, this confirmed my first opinion, that a people who could so far civilize brute animals must needs excel in wisdom all the nations of the world. The gray came in just after, and thereby prevented any ill treatment which the others might have given me. He neighed to them several times in a style of authority, and received answers.

Beyond this room there were three others, reaching the length of the house, to which you passed through three doors, opposite to each other, in the manner of a vista. We went through the second room toward the third. Here the gray walked in first, beckoning me to attend. I waited in the second room, and got ready my presents for the master and mistress of the house. They were two knives, three bracelets of false pearl, a small looking glass, and a bead necklace. The horse neighed three or four times, and I waited to hear some answers in a human voice, but I heard no other returns than in the same dialect, only one or two a little shriller than his.

I began to think that this house must belong to some person of great note among them, because there appeared so much ceremony before I could gain admittance. But that a man of quality should be served all by horses was beyond my comprehension. I feared my brain was disturbed by my sufferings and misfortunes.

I roused myself, and looked about me in the room where I was left alone. This was furnished like the first, only after a more elegant manner. I rubbed my eyes often, but the same objects still occurred. I pinched my arms and sides to awake myself, hoping I might be in a dream. I then absolutely concluded that all these appearances could be nothing else but necromancy and magic. But I had no time to pursue these reflections, for the gray horse came to the door and made me a sign to follow him into the third room, where I saw a very comely mare, together with a colt and foal, sitting on their haunches upon mats of straw, not unartfully made, and perfectly neat and clean.

The mare, soon after my entrance, rose from her mat, and coming up close, after having nicely observed my hands and face, gave me a most contemp-

tuous look. Then turning to the horse, I heard the
word *Yahoo* often repeated betwixt them; the meaning of which word I could not then comprehend, although it was the first I had learned to pronounce.
But I was soon better informed, to my everlasting
mortification. For the horse, beckoning to me with
his head, and repeating the word *hhuun, hhuun,* as
he did upon the road, which I understood was to attend him, led me out into a kind of court, where was
another building at some distance from the house.

Here we entered, and I saw three of these detestable creatures, whom I first met after my landing,
feeding upon roots, and the flesh of some animals,

which I afterward found to be that of asses and dogs, and now and then a cow dead by accident or disease. They were all tied by the neck with strong withes, fastened to a beam. They held their food between the claws of their forefeet, and tore it with their teeth.

The master horse ordered a sorrel nag, one of his servants, to untie the largest of these animals, and take him into the yard. The beast and I were brought close together, and our countenances diligently compared, both by master and servant, who thereupon repeated several times the word *Yahoo*. My horror and astonishment are not to be described, when I observed in this abominable animal a perfect human figure. The face of it indeed was flat and broad, the nose depressed, the lips large, and the mouth wide.

The forefeet of the Yahoo differed from my hands in nothing else but the length of the nails, the coarseness and brownness of the palms, and the hairiness on the backs. There was the same resemblance between our feet, with the same differences, which I knew very well, though the horses did not, because of my shoes and stockings; the same in every part of our bodies, except as to hairiness and color, which I have already described.

The great difficulty that seemed to stick with the two horses was to see the rest of my body so very different from that of a Yahoo, for which I was obliged

The beast and I were brought close together

to my clothes, whereof they had no conception. The sorrel nag offered me a root, which he held between his hoof and pastern. I took it in my hand, and having smelt it, returned it to him again as civilly as I could. He brought out of the Yahoo's kennel a piece of ass's flesh, but it smelt so offensively that I turned from it with loathing. He then threw it to the Yahoo, by whom it was greedily devoured. He afterward showed me a wisp of hay, and a fetlock full of oats. But I shook my head, to signify that neither of these were food for me.

And indeed, I now apprehended that I must absolutely starve if I did not get to some of my own species. As to those filthy Yahoos, although there were few greater lovers of mankind, at that time, than myself, yet I confess I never saw any sensitive being so detestable on all accounts; and the more I came near them the more hateful they grew, while I stayed in that country. This the master horse observed by my behavior, and therefore sent the Yahoo back to his kennel.

He then put his forehoof to his mouth, at which I was much surprised, although he did it with ease, and with a motion that appeared perfectly natural, and made other signs to know what I would eat. But I could not return him such an answer as he was able to apprehend. And if he had understood me, I did not see how it was possible to contrive any way for finding myself nourishment. While we were thus engaged, I observed a cow passing by, whereupon I pointed to her, and expressed a desire to let me go and milk her. This had its effect. He led me back into the house, and ordered a mare-servant to open a room, where a good store of milk lay in earthen and wooden vessels, after a very orderly and cleanly manner. She gave me a large bowlful, of which I drank very heartily and found myself well refreshed.

About noon I saw coming toward the house a kind of vehicle, drawn like a sledge by four Yahoos. There was in it an old steed, who seemed to be of quality. He alighted with his hind feet forward, having by accident got a hurt in his left forefoot. He came to dine with our horse, who received him with great civility. They dined in the best room, and had oats boiled in milk for the second course, which the old horse ate warm, but the rest cold.

Their mangers were placed circular in the middle of the room, and divided into several partitions, round which they sat on their haunches upon bosses of straw. In the middle was a large rack with angles answering to every partition of the manger; so that each horse and mare ate their own hay, and their own mash of oats and milk, with much decency and regularity. The behavior of the young colt and foal appeared very modest, and that of the master and mistress extremely cheerful and complaisant to their

guest. The gray ordered me to stand by him, and much discourse passed between him and his friend concerning me, as I found by the stranger's often looking on me, and the frequent repetition of the word *Yahoo*.

I happened to wear my gloves, which the master gray, observing, seemed perplexed, showing signs of wonder what I had done to my forefeet. He put his hoof three or four times to them, as if he would signify that I should reduce them to their former shape, which I presently did, pulling off both my gloves, and putting them into my pocket. This occasioned further talk, and I saw the company was pleased with my behavior, whereof I soon found the good effects. I was ordered to speak the few words I understood, and while they were at dinner the master taught me the names for oats, milk, fire, water, and some others; which I could readily pronounce after him, having from my youth a great facility in learning languages.

When dinner was done the master horse took me aside, and by signs and words made me understand the concern that he was in because I had nothing to eat. Oats in their tongue are called *hlunnh*. This word I pronounced two or three times. For although I had refused them at first, yet upon second thoughts I considered that I could contrive to make of them a kind of bread, which might be sufficient with milk to keep me alive till I could make my escape to some other country and to creatures of my own spec es.

The horse immediately ordered a white mare-servant of his family to bring me a good quantity of oats in a sort of wooden tray. These I heated before the fire as well as I could, and rubbed them till the husks came off, which I made a shift to winnow from the grain. I ground and beat them between two stones, then took water, and made them into a paste or cake, which I toasted at the fire, and ate warm with milk. It was at first a very insipid diet, though common enough in many parts of Europe, but grew tolerable by time. And having been often reduced to hard fare in my life, this was not the first experiment I had made how easily nature is satisfied. And I cannot but observe that I never had one hour's sickness while I stayed in this island.

I sometimes made a shift to catch a rabbit or bird by snares made of Yahoos' hairs, and I often gathered wholesome herbs, which I boiled, or ate as salads with my bread, and now and then, for a rarity, I made a little butter, and drank the whey. I was at first at a great loss for salt, but custom soon reconciled the want of it; and I am confident that the frequent use of salt among us is an effect of luxury.

When it grew toward evening, the master horse ordered a place for me to lodge in. It was but six yards from the house, and separated from the stable of the Yahoos. Here I got some straw and, covering myself with my own clothes, slept very sound.

CHAPTER 20

Gulliver Understands the
Speech of the Master Horse

MY PRINCIPAL ENDEAVOR was to learn the language, which my master (for so I shall henceforth call him) and his children and every servant of his house were desirous to teach me. For they looked upon it as a prodigy that a brute animal should discover such marks of a rational creature. I pointed to everything and inquired the name of it, which I wrote down in my journal book when I was alone, and corrected my bad accent by desiring those of the family to pronounce it often. In this employment, a sorrel nag, one of the underservants, was ready to assist me.

The curiosity and impatience of my master were so great that he spent many hours of his leisure to instruct me. He was convinced (as he afterward told me) that I must be a Yahoo, but my teachableness, civility, and cleanliness astonished him; which were qualities altogether so opposite to those animals. He was most perplexed about my clothes, reasoning sometimes with himself whether they were a part of my body, for I never pulled them off till the family were asleep and got them on before they waked in

the morning. My master was eager to learn from where I came, how I acquired those appearances of reason which I showed in all my actions, and to know my story from my own mouth, which he hoped he should soon do by the great proficiency I made in learning and pronouncing their words and sentences.

In about ten weeks' time I was able to understand most of his questions, and in three months could give him some tolerable answers. He was extremely curious to know from what part of the country I came, and how I was taught to imitate a rational creature; because the Yahoos (whom he saw I exactly resembled in my head, hands, and face), with some appearance of cunning, and the strongest disposition to mischief, were observed to be the most unteachable of all brutes. I answered that I came over the sea from a far place, with many others of my own kind, in a great hollow vessel made of the bodies of trees; that my companions forced me to land on this coast, and then left me to shift for myself. It was with some difficulty, and by the help of many signs, that I brought him to understand me.

He replied, that I must needs be mistaken, or that I *said the thing which was not.* (For they have no word in their language to express lying or falsehood.) He knew it was impossible that there could be a country beyond the sea, or that a parcel of brutes could move a wooden vessel whither they pleased upon water. He was sure no Houyhnhnm alive could make such a vessel, nor would trust Yahoos to manage it.

I told my master that I was at a loss for expression, but would improve as fast as I could; and hoped in a short time I should be able to tell him wonders. He was pleased to direct his own mare, his colt and foal, and the servants of the family, to take all opportunities of instructing me, and every day for two or three hours he was at the same pains himself. Several horses and mares of quality in the neighborhood came often to our house upon the report spread of a wonderful Yahoo that could speak like a Houyhnhnm and seemed in his words and actions to show some glimmerings of reason. These delighted to converse with me. They put many questions, and received such answers as I was able to return. By all these advantages I made so great a progress that in five months from my arrival I understood whatever was spoke and could express myself tolerably well.

The Houyhnhnms who came to visit my master with the design of seeing and talking with me, could hardly believe me to be a right Yahoo, because my body had a different covering from others of my kind. They were astonished to observe me without the usual hair or skin, except on my head, face, and hands; but I discovered that secret to my master, upon an accident which happened about a fortnight before.

I have already told the reader, that every night

when the family were gone to bed it was my custom to strip and cover myself with my clothes. It happened one morning early that my master sent for me by the sorrel nag, who was his valet; when he came I was fast asleep, my clothes fallen off on one side, and my shirt above my waist. I awakened at the noise he made, and observed him to deliver his message in some disorder; after which he went to my master, and in a great fright gave him a very confused account of what he had seen. This I presently discovered; for going as soon as I was dressed to pay my at-

tendance upon his Honor, he asked me the meaning
of what his servant had reported, that I was not the
same thing when I slept as I appeared to be at other
times; that his valet assured him, some part of me
was white, some yellow, at least not so white, and
some brown.

I had hitherto concealed the secret of my dress, in
order to distinguish myself as much as possible from
that cursed race of Yahoos; but now I found it in vain
to do so any longer. Besides, I considered that my
clothes and shoes would soon wear out, which already were in a declining condition, and must be
supplied by some contrivance from the hides of Yahoos or other brutes; whereby the whole secret would
be known. I therefore told my master that in the
country from which I came those of my kind always
covered their bodies with the hairs of certain animals
prepared by art, as well for decency as to avoid the
inclemencies of air, both hot and cold; of which, as to
my own person, I would give him immediate convic-
tion, if he pleased to command me; only desiring his
excuse, if I did not expose those parts that nature
taught us to conceal. He said my discourse was all
very strange, but especially the last part; for he could
not understand why nature should teach us to conceal what nature had given. That neither himself nor
family were ashamed of any parts of their bodies;
but however I might do as I pleased. Whereupon I

first unbuttoned my coat and pulled it off. I did the same with my waistcoat; I drew off my shoes, stockings, and breeches. I let my shirt down to my waist, and drew up the bottom, fastening it like a girdle about my middle.

My master observed the whole performance with great signs of curiosity and admiration. He took up all my clothes in his pastern, one piece after another, and examined them diligently; he then stroked my body very gently and looked round me several times, after which he said it was plain I must be a perfect

Yahoo; but that I differed very much from the rest of my species, in the softness and whiteness and smoothness of my skin, my want of hair in several parts of my body, the shape and shortness of my claws behind and before, and my affectation of walking continually on my two hind feet. He desired to see no more, and gave me leave to put on my clothes again, for I was shuddering with cold.

I expressed my uneasiness at his giving me so often the appellation of Yahoo, an odious animal for which I had so utter a hatred and contempt. I begged he would forbear applying that word to me, and take the same order in his family, and among his friends whom he suffered to see me. I requested likewise that the secret of my having a false covering to my body might be known to none but himself, at least as long as my present clothing should last; for as to what the sorrel nag his valet had observed, his Honor might command him to conceal it.

All this my master very graciously consented to, and thus the secret was kept till my clothes began to wear out, which I was forced to supply by several contrivances that shall hereafter be mentioned. In the meantime he desired I would go on with my utmost diligence to learn their language, because he was more astonished at my capacity for speech and reason than at the figure of my body, whether it were covered or not; adding that he waited with some impatience to hear the wonders which I promised to tell him.

From thenceforward he doubled the pains he had been at to instruct me; he brought me into all company, and made them treat me with civility, because, as he told them privately, this would put me into good humor and make me more diverting.

Every day when I waited on him, besides the trouble he was at in teaching, he would ask me several questions concerning myself, which I answered as well as I could.

I explained that I came from a very far country with about fifty more of my own species; that we traveled upon the seas, in a great hollow vessel made of wood, and larger than his Honor's house. I described the ship to him in the best terms I could, and explained by the help of my handkerchief displayed, how it was driven forward by the wind. I said that after a quarrel among us I was set on shore on this coast, where I walked forward without knowing whither, till he delivered me from the persecution of those execrable Yahoos.

He asked me who made the ship, and how it was possible that the Houyhnhnms of my country would leave it to the management of brutes. My answer was that I dare proceed no further in my relation unless he would give me his word and honor that he would not be offended, and then I would tell him the wonders I had so often promised.

He agreed; and I went on by assuring him that the ship was made by creatures like myself, who in all the countries I had traveled, as well as in my own, were the only governing, rational animals; and that upon my arrival here I was as much astonished to see the Houyhnhnms act like rational beings as he or his friends could be in finding some marks of reason in a creature he was pleased to call a Yahoo, to which I owned my resemblance in every part but could not account for their degenerate and brutal nature.

I said further that if good fortune ever restored me to my native country, to relate my travels here, everybody would believe that I *said the thing which was not;* that I invented the story out of my own head. And with all possible respect to himself, his family and friends, and under his promise of not being offended, our countrymen would hardly think it probable that a Houyhnhnm should be the presiding creature of a nation and a Yahoo the brute.

When I asserted that the Yahoos were the only governing animals in my country, which my master said was altogether past his conception, he desired to know whether we had Houyhnhnms among us, and what was their employment. I told him we had great numbers, that in summer they grazed in the

fields, and in winter were kept in houses, with hay and oats, where Yahoo servants were employed to rub their skins smooth, comb their manes, serve them with food, and make their beds.

"I understand you well," said my master, "it is now very plain, from all you have spoken, that whatever share of reason the Yahoos pretend to, the Houyhnhnms are your masters. I heartily wish our Yahoos would be so tractable."

I begged his Honor would please to excuse me from proceeding any further, because I was very certain that the account he expected from me would be highly displeasing. But he insisted in commanding me to let him know the best and the worst. I told him he should be obeyed. I owned that the Houyhnhnms among us, whom we called horses, were the most generous and comely animals we had, that they excelled in strength and swiftness. And when they belonged to persons of quality, employed in traveling, racing, or drawing chariots, they were treated with much kindness and care, till they fell into diseases or became foundered in the feet. Then they were sold, and used to all kind of drudgery till they died; after which their skins were stripped and sold for what they were worth, and their bodies left to be devoured by dogs and birds of prey.

But the common race of horses had not so good fortune, being kept by farmers and carriers, and other mean people, who put them to great labor, and fed them worse. I described, as well as I could, our way of riding, the shape and use of a bridle, a saddle, a spur, and a whip, of harness and wheels. I added that we fastened plates of a certain hard substance called iron at the bottom of their feet, to preserve their hoofs from being broken by the stony ways on which we often traveled.

My master, after some expressions of great indignation, wondered how we dared to venture upon a Houyhnhnm's back, for he was sure that the weakest servant in his house would be able to shake off the strongest Yahoo, or by lying down and rolling on his back squeeze the brute to death. I answered that our horses were trained up from three or four years old to the several uses we intended them for; that if any of them proved intolerably vicious, they were employed for carriages; that they were severely beaten while they were young, for any mischievous tricks; that they were indeed sensible of rewards and punishments. But his Honor would please to consider that they had not the least tincture of reason any more than the Yahoos in this country.

It put me to the pains of many circumlocutions to give my master a right idea of what I spoke, for their language does not abound in variety of words because their wants and passions are fewer than among us. But it is impossible to represent his noble resentment at our savage treatment of the Houyhnhnm race.

He said if it were possible there could be any country where Yahoos alone were endowed with reason, they certainly must be the governing animal, because reason will in time always prevail against brutal strength. But considering the frame of our bodies, and especially of mine, he thought no creature of equal bulk was so ill contrived for employing that reason in the common offices of life. Whereupon he desired to know whether those among whom I lived resembled me or the Yahoos of his country. I assured him that I was as well shaped as most of my age; but the younger and the females were much more soft and tender, and the skins of the latter generally as white as milk.

He said I differed indeed from other Yahoos, being much more cleanly, and not altogether so deformed, but in point of real advantage he thought I differed for the worse: that my nails were of no use either to my fore or hind feet. As to my forefeet, he could not properly call them by that name, for he never observed me to walk upon them; that they were too soft to bear the ground; that I generally went with them uncovered, neither was the covering I sometimes wore on them of the same shape or so strong as that on my feet behind.

He then began to find fault with other parts of my body: the flatness of my face, the prominence of my nose, my eyes placed directly in front, so that I could not look on either side without turning my head; that I was not able to feed myself without lifting one of my forefeet to my mouth; and therefore nature had placed these joints to answer that necessity. He knew not what could be the use of those several clefts and divisions in my feet behind; that these were too soft to bear the hardness and sharpness of stones without a covering made from the skin of some other brute; that my whole body wanted a fence against heat and

cold, which I was forced to put on and off every day
with tediousness and trouble. However, he said he
would debate the matter no further, because he was
more desirous to know my own story, the country
where I was born, and the several actions and events
of my life before I came here.

I said my birth was of honest parents in an island
called England, governed by a female whom we
called a queen. I was bred a surgeon, whose trade it
is to cure wounds and hurts in the body, got by accident or violence. I left home to get riches, whereby
I might maintain myself and family when I should
return. In my last voyage I was commander of the
ship and had about fifty Yahoos under me, many of
whom died at sea, and I was forced to replace them
by others picked out from several nations. Our ship
was twice in danger of being sunk: the first time by a
great storm, and the second by striking against a
rock.

Here my master interposed, asking me how I could
persuade strangers out of different countries to venture with me, after the losses I had sustained and the
hazards I had run. I said they were fellows of desperate fortunes, forced to fly from the places of their
birth on account of their poverty or their crimes;
none of whom dared return to their native countries
for fear of being hanged or of starving in a jail, and

therefore were under the necessity of seeking a livelihood in other places.

During this discourse my master was pleased to

interrupt me several times. I had made use of roundabout language in describing to him the nature of the several crimes for which most of our crew had been forced to fly their country. This labor took up several days' conversation before he was able to

comprehend me. He was wholly at a loss to know
what could be the use or necessity of practicing those
vices. I endeavored to give some ideas of the desire
of power and riches, of the terrible effects of intemperance, malice, and envy. All this I was forced to
define and describe by the putting of cases. After
which, like one whose imagination was struck with
something never seen or heard of before, he would
lift up his eyes with amazement and indignation.
Power, government, war, law, punishment, and a
thousand other things had no terms wherein his language could express them, which made it difficult to
give my master any conception of what I meant.

CHAPTER 21

Gulliver Discusses England & Makes

Observations on the Houyhnhnms

THE FOLLOWING EXTRACT of many conversations I had with my master contains the most material points which were discoursed at several times for above two years; his Honor often desiring fuller satisfaction as I further improved in the Houyhnhnm tongue. I laid before him, as well as I could, the whole state of Europe; I discoursed of trade and manufactures, of arts and sciences; and the answers I gave to all the questions he made, as they arose upon several subjects, were a fund of conversation not to be exhausted.

I told him about the revolution under the Prince of Orange and about the long war with France wherein the greatest powers of Christendom were engaged. I computed that about a million Yahoos might have been killed in the whole progress of it, and perhaps a hundred or more cities taken, and thrice as many ships burnt or sunk.

He asked me what were the usual causes or motives that made one country go to war with another. I answered they were innumerable, but I should only mention a few of the chief. Sometimes the ambition of princes, who never think they have land or people enough to govern; sometimes the corruption of ministers, who engage their master in a war in order to stifle or divert the clamor of the subjects against their evil administration. Difference in opinions has cost many millions of lives.

Sometimes the quarrel between two princes is to decide which of them shall dispossess a third of his dominions, where neither of them pretends to any right. Sometimes one prince quarrels with another, for fear the other should quarrel with him. Sometimes a war is entered upon because the enemy is too strong, and sometimes because he is too weak. Sometimes our neighbors want the things which we have, or have the things which we want; and we both fight, till they take ours or give us theirs.

"What you have told me," said my master, "upon the subject of war does indeed show most admirably the effects of that reason you pretend to. However, it is happy that the shame is greater than the danger; and that nature has left you utterly uncapable of doing much mischief.

"For your mouths lying flat with your faces, you can hardly bite each other to any purpose, unless by

consent. Then as to the claws upon your feet before and behind, they are so short and tender that one of our Yahoos would drive a dozen of yours before him. And therefore in recounting the numbers of those who have been killed in battle, I cannot but think that you have *said the thing which is not*."

I could not forbear shaking my head and smiling a little at his ignorance. And being no stranger to the

art of war, I gave him a description of cannons, mus-
kets, pistols, bullets, powder, swords, bayonets, bat-
tles, sieges, retreats, attacks, undermines, counter-
mines, bombardments, sea fights; ships sunk with a
thousand men, twenty thousand killed on each side;
dying groans, trampling to death under horses' feet;
flight, pursuit, victory; plundering, stripping, burning, and destroying. And to set forth the valor of my
own dear countrymen, I assured him that I had seen
them blow up a hundred enemies at once in a siege,
and as many in a ship.

I was going on to more particulars, when my master commanded me silence. He said whoever understood the nature of Yahoos might easily believe it
possible for so vile an animal to be capable of every
action I had named, if their strength and cunning
equaled their malice.

He added that he had heard too much upon the
subject of war, both in this and some former discourses. There was another point which a little perplexed him at present. I had informed him that some
of our crew left their country on account of being
ruined by law; that I had already explained the
meaning of the word; but he was at a loss how it
should come to pass that the law, which was intended for every man's preservation, should be any
man's ruin.

I said there was a society of men among us, bred

up from their youth in the art of proving that white is black, and black is white, according as they are paid. To this society all the rest of the people are slaves. "For example, if my neighbor has a mind to my cow, he hires a lawyer to prove that he ought to have my cow from me. I must then hire another to defend my right, it being against all rules of law that any man should be allowed to speak for himself.

"In pleading they studiously avoid entering into the merits of the cause, but are loud, violent, and tedious in dwelling upon all circumstances which are not to the purpose. For instance, in the case already mentioned, they never desire to know what claim or title my adversary has to my cow; but whether the said cow were red or black, her horns long or short, whether the field I graze her in be round or square, whether she was milked at home or abroad, what diseases she is subject to, and the like. After this they adjourn the cause from time to time, and perhaps in ten, twenty, or thirty years come to an issue."

My master was yet wholly at a loss to understand what motives could incite this race of lawyers to perplex and weary themselves, and engage in a confederacy of injustice, merely for the sake of injuring their fellow animals; neither could he comprehend what I meant in saying they did it for hire. Whereupon I was at much pains to describe to him the use of money, the materials it was made of, and the value

of the metals; that when a Yahoo had got a great
store of this precious substance, he was able to purchase whatever he had a mind to: the finest clothing,
the noblest houses, great tracts of land, the most
costly meats and drinks. Therefore since money
alone was able to perform
all these feats, our Yahoos
thought they could never
have enough of it to spend or
save. The rich man enjoyed

the fruit of the poor man's labor, and the latter were
a thousand to one in proportion to the former. That
the bulk of our people were forced to live miserably,
by laboring every day for small wages to make a few
live plentifully.

His Honor was still perplexed, for he believed that
all animals had a title to their share in the produc-
tions of the earth, and especially those who presided
over the rest. Therefore he desired to know what
these costly meats were, and how any of us happened to want them. Whereupon I enumerated as
many sorts as came into my head, with the various
methods of dressing them, which could not be done
without sending vessels by sea to every part of the
world, as well for liquors to drink as for sauces and
innumerable other conveniences.

I assured him that this whole globe of earth must
be at least three times gone round before one of our
better female Yahoos could get her breakfast or a
cup to put it in. He said that must needs be a miserable country which cannot furnish food for its own
inhabitants. But what he chiefly wondered at was
how such vast tracts of ground as I described should
be wholly without fresh water, and the people put to
the necessity of sending over the sea for drink.

I replied that England (the dear place of my na-
tivity) was computed to produce three times the
quantity of food that its inhabitants are able to con-

sume, as well as liquors extracted from grain or pressed out of the fruit of certain trees, which made excellent drink, and the same proportion in every other convenience of life. But, in order to feed the luxury and intemperance of the males, and the vanity of the females, we sent away the greatest part of our necessary things to other countries, from whence in return we brought the materials of diseases, folly, and vice, to spend among ourselves.

I explained that wine was not imported among us from foreign countries, to supply the want of water or other drinks, but because it was a sort of liquid which made us merry by putting us out of our senses, diverted all melancholy thoughts, raised our hopes, and banished our fears, suspended every office of reason for a time, and deprived us of the use of our limbs, till we fell into a profound sleep; although it must be confessed, that we always awoke sick and dispirited and that the use of this liquor filled us with diseases, which made our lives uncomfortable and short.

But besides all this, the bulk of our people supported themselves by furnishing the necessities or conveniences of life to the rich, and to each other. "For instance," I said, "when I am at home and dressed as I ought to be, I carry on my body the workmanship of a hundred tradesmen. The building and furniture of my house employ as many more, and five times the number to adorn my wife."

I was going on to tell him of another sort of people, who get their livelihood by attending the sick, having upon some occasions informed his Honor that many of my crew had died of diseases. But here it was with the utmost difficulty that I brought him to apprehend what I meant. He could easily conceive that a Houyhnhnm grew weak and heavy a few days before his death, or by some accident might hurt a limb. But that nature, who works all things to perfection, should suffer any pains to breed in our bodies, he thought impossible, and desired to know the reason of so unaccountable an evil. I told him we fed on a thousand things which operated contrary to each other; that we ate when we were not hungry, and drank without the provocation of thirst; that we sat whole nights drinking strong liquors without eating a bit, which disposed us to sloth, inflamed our bodies, and precipitated or prevented digestion. To remedy which there was a sort of people bred up among us, in the profession or pretense of curing the sick.

I must freely confess that the many virtues of those excellent quadrupeds placed in opposite view to human corruptions had so far opened my eyes and enlarged my understanding that I began to view the actions and passions of man in a very different light, and to think the honor of my own kind not worth managing. Besides, it was impossible for me to do so before a person of so acute a judgment as my

master, who daily convinced me of a thousand faults
in myself, whereof I had not the least perception before, and which among us would never be numbered
even among human infirmities. I had likewise
learned from his example an utter detestation of all
falsehood or disguise, and truth appeared so amiable
to me, that I determined upon sacrificing everything to it.

I had not been a year in this country before I con-
tracted such a love and veneration for the inhab-

The youth meet to show their proficiency in running and leaping

itants that I entered on a firm resolution never to return to human kind, but to pass the rest of my life among these admirable Houyhnhnms in the contemplation and practice of every virtue; where I could have no example or incitement to vice. But it was decreed by fortune, my perpetual enemy, that so great a felicity should not fall to my share.

My master made many comparisons between me and the Yahoos, often to my disadvantage. And our reasons for waging war seemed no more valid to him than the causes of quarrels among the Yahoos: they fought over food and shining stones found in the fields, which they hoarded as Europeans hoarded wealth.

As I ought to have understood human nature much better than I supposed it possible for my master to do, so it was easy to apply the character he gave of the Yahoos to myself and my countrymen. And I believed I could yet make further discoveries from my own observation. I therefore often begged him to let me go among the herds of Yahoos in the neighborhood, to which he always very graciously consented. He ordered one of his servants, a strong sorrel nag, very honest and good-natured, to be my guard, without whose protection I dare not undertake such adventures.

By what I could discover, the Yahoos appear to be the most unteachable of all animals, their capacities never reaching higher than to draw or carry burdens. Yet I am of opinion this defect arises chiefly from a perverse disposition. For they are cunning, malicious, treacherous, and revengeful. They are strong and hardy, but of a cowardly spirit, and by consequence, insolent, abject, and cruel. It is observed that the red-haired of both sexes much exceed the rest in strength and activity.

The Houyhnhnms keep the Yahoos for present use in huts not far from the house. But the rest are sent abroad to certain fields, where they dig up roots, eat several kinds of herbs, and sometimes catch weasels and wild rats which they greedily devour. Nature has taught them to dig deep holes with their nails on the side of a rising ground, wherein they lie by themselves. The kennels of the females are larger, sufficient to hold two or three cubs. They swim from their infancy like frogs, and are able to continue long underwater, where they often take fish, which the females carry home to their young.

Having lived three years in this country, the reader I suppose will expect that I should, like other travelers, give him some account of the manners and customs of its inhabitants, which it was indeed my principal study to learn.

Friendship and benevolence are the two principal virtues among the Houyhnhnms, and these not confined to particular objects, but universal to the whole race. For a stranger from the remotest part is equally treated with the nearest neighbor, and wherever he goes looks upon himself as at home. They preserve decency and civility in the highest degrees, but are altogether ignorant of ceremony. They have no fondness for their colts or foals, but the care they take in educating them proceeds entirely from the dictates of reason. And I observed my master to show the same affection to his neighbor's issue that he had for his own. They will have it that nature teaches them to love the whole species, and it is reason only that makes a distinction of persons, where there is a superior degree of virtue.

In educating the youth of both sexes, their method is admirable, and highly deserves our imitation. These are not suffered to taste a grain of oats, except upon certain days, till eighteen years old; nor milk, but very rarely; and in summer they graze two hours in the morning, and as long in the evening. But the servants are not allowed above half that time, and a great part of their grass is brought home, which they eat at the most convenient hours, when they can be best spared from work.

Temperance, industry, exercise, and cleanliness are the lessons equally enjoined to the young ones of both sexes. My master thought it monstrous in us to give the females a different kind of education from the males, except in some articles of domestic management.

The Houyhnhnms train up their youth to strength,

speed, and hardiness, by exercising them in running races up and down steep hills, and over hard stony grounds. When they are all in a sweat, they are ordered to leap over head and ears into a pond or river. Four times a year the youth of a certain district meet to show their proficiency in running and leaping, and other feats of strength and agility; where the victor is rewarded with a song made in his or her praise.

Every fourth year, in the spring, there is a representative council of the whole nation, which meets in a plain about twenty miles from our house, and continues about five or six days. Here they inquire into the state and condition of the several districts; whether they abound or be deficient in hay or oats, or cows or Yahoos. And wherever there is any want (which is seldom) it is immediately supplied by unanimous consent and contribution.

The Houyhnhnms have no letters, and consequently their knowledge is all traditional. But there being few events of any moment among a people so well united, naturally disposed to every virtue, wholly governed by reason, and cut off from all commerce with other nations, the historical part is easily preserved without burdening their memories. I have already observed that they are subject to no diseases, and therefore can have no need of physicians. However, they have excellent medicines composed of herbs, to cure accidental bruises and cuts.

They calculate the year by the revolution of the sun and the moon, but use no subdivisions into weeks. They are well enough acquainted with the motions of those two heavenly bodies, and understand the nature of eclipses; and this is the utmost progress of their astronomy.

In poetry they must be allowed to excel all other mortals. Their verses usually contain either some exalted notions of friendship and benevolence or the praises of those who were victors in races and other bodily exercises.

Their buildings, although very rude and simple, are not inconvenient, but well contrived to defend them from all injuries of cold and heat. They have a kind of tree, which at forty years old loosens in the root, and falls with the first storm. These trees grow very straight, and being pointed like stakes with a sharp stone (for the Houyhnhnms know not the use of iron), they stick them erect in the ground about ten inches apart, and then weave in oat straw, or sometimes wattles betwixt them. The roof is made after the same maner, and so are the doors.

The Houyhnhnms use the hollow part between the pastern and the hoof of their forefeet as we do our hands, and this with greater dexterity than I could at first imagine. I have seen a white mare of our family thread a needle (which I lent her on purpose) with that joint. They milk their cows, reap their oats, and do all the work which requires hands, in the same manner. They have a kind of hard flints, which by grinding against other stones they form into instruments, that serve instead of wedges, axes, and hammers. With tools made of these flints they likewise cut their hay and reap their oats. The Yahoos draw home the sheaves in carriages, and the servants tread them in certain covered huts, to get out the

grain, which is kept in stores. They make a rude kind of earthen and wooden vessels, and bake the former in the sun.

If they can avoid casualties, they die only of old age, and are buried in the most obscure places that can be found, their friends and relations expressing neither joy nor grief at their departure. Nor does the dying person discover the least regret that he is leaving the world, any more than if he were upon returning home from a visit to one of his neighbors. I remember my master having once made an appointment with a friend and his family to come to his house upon some affair of importance. On the day fixed the mistress and her two children came very late. She made two excuses, first for her husband, who, as she said, happened that very morning to *shnuwnh*. The word is strongly expressive in their language, but not easily rendered into English; it signifies "to retire to his first mother." Her excuse for not coming sooner was that, her husband dying late in the morning, she was a good while consulting her servants about a convenient place where his body should be laid. I observed she behaved herself at our house as cheerfully as the rest, and died about three months after.

They live generally to seventy or seventy-five years, very seldom to fourscore. Some weeks before their death they feel a gradual decay, but without pain. During this time they are much visited by their friends, because they cannot go abroad with their usual ease and satisfaction. However, about ten days before their death, which they seldom fail in computing, they return the visits that have been made them by those who are nearest in the neighborhood, being carried in a convenient sledge drawn by Yahoos. This vehicle they use, not only upon this occasion, but when they grow old, upon long journeys, or when they are lamed by any accident. And therefore when the dying Houyhnhnms return those visits, they take a solemn leave of their friends, as if they were going to some remote part of the country, where they designed to pass the rest of their lives.

I could with great pleasure enlarge further upon the manners and virtues of this excellent people, but must close upon that subject and proceed to relate my own sad catastrophe.

CHAPTER 22

Gulliver Is Forced

to Return Home

I HAD SETTLED my little economy to my own heart's content. My master had ordered a room to be made for me after their manner, about six yards from the house; the sides and floors of which I plastered with clay, and covered with rush-mats of my own contriving. I had beaten hemp, which there grows wild, and made of it a sort of ticking. This I filled with the feathers of several birds I had taken with snares, and were excellent food. I had fashioned two chairs with my knife, the sorrel nag helping me in the more laborious part.

When my clothes were worn to rags, I made myself others with the skins of rabbits and of a certain beautiful animal about the same size, the skin of which is covered with a fine down. Of these I likewise made very tolerable stockings. I soled my shoes with wood which I cut from a tree and fitted to the upper leather; when this was worn out, I supplied it with skins dried in the sun. I often got honey out of hollow trees, which I mingled with water, or ate with my bread. No man could more verify the truth of these two maxims: "Nature is very easily satisfied" and "Necessity is the mother of invention."

I enjoyed perfect health of body and tranquillity of mind. I did not feel the treachery or inconstancy of a friend, nor the injuries of a secret or open enemy.

I had the favor of being admitted to several Houyhnhnms, who came to visit or dine with my master; where his Honor graciously suffered me to

wait in the room, and listen to their discourse. Both he and his company would often descend to ask me questions, and receive my answers. I had also sometimes the honor of attending my master in his visits to others. I never presumed to speak, except in answer to a question. No person spoke without being pleased himself, and pleasing his companions; there was no interruption, heat, or difference of sentiments.

I freely confess that all the little knowledge I have of any value was acquired by the lectures I received from my master, and from hearing the discourses of him and his friends. I admired the strength, comeliness, and speed of the inhabitants; and such a constellation of virtues in such amiable persons produced in me the highest veneration.

When I thought of my family, my friends, my countrymen, or human race in general, I considered them as they really were: Yahoos in shape and disposition, perhaps a little more civilized, and qualified with the gift of speech, but making no other use of reason than to improve and multiply their vices. When I happened to behold the reflection of my own form in a lake or fountain, I turned away my face in horror and detestation of myself and could better endure the sight of a common Yahoo than of my own person.

By conversing with the Houyhnhnms, and looking

upon them with delight, I fell to imitate their gait and gesture, which is now grown into a habit, and my friends often tell me in a blunt way that I trot like a horse; which, however, I take for a great compliment. In speaking I am apt to fall into the voice and manner of the Houyhnhnms, and hear myself ridiculed on that account without the least mortification.

In the midst of all this happiness, and when I looked upon myself to be fully settled for life, my master sent for me one morning a little earlier than his usual hour. I observed by his countenance that he was in some perplexity, and at a loss how to begin what he had to speak. After a short silence he told me he did not know how I would take what he was going to say: in the last general assembly, when the affair of the Yahoos was entered upon, the representatives had taken offense at his keeping a Yahoo (meaning myself) in his family more like a Houyhnhnm than a brute animal. He was known frequently to converse with me, as if he could receive some advantage or pleasure in my company. Such a practice was not agreeable to reason or nature, nor a thing ever heard of before among them.

The assembly did therefore exhort him either to employ me like the rest of my species or command me to swim back to the place from where I came. The first of these expedients was utterly rejected by all the Houyhnhnms who had ever seen me at his house or their own. For they alleged that because I had some rudiments of reason, it was to be feared I might be able to seduce them into the woody and mountainous parts of the country and foment a revolt.

My master added that he was daily pressed by the Houyhnhnms of the neighborhood to have the assembly's edict executed, which he could not put off much longer. He doubted it would be impossible for me to swim to another country, and therefore wished I would contrive some sort of vehicle resembling those I had described to him, that might carry me on the sea; in which work I should have the assistance of his own servants, as well as those of his neighbors. He concluded that for his own part he could have been content to keep me in his service as long as I lived.

I was struck with the utmost grief and despair at my master's discourse, and being unable to support the agonies I was under, I fell into a swoon at his feet. When I came to myself he told me that he concluded I had been dead (for these people are subject to no such weakness). I answered in a faint voice that death would have been too great a happiness; that although I could not blame the assembly's edict, or the urgency of his friends, yet, in my weak and corrupt judgment, I thought it might consist with reason to have been less rigorous.

I could not swim a league, and probably the nearest land to theirs might be distant above a hundred. Many materials necessary for making a small vessel to carry me off were wholly wanting in this country, which, however, I would attempt in obedience and gratitude to his Honor, although I concluded the thing to be impossible, and therefore looked on myself as already devoted to destruction. That the certain prospect of an unnatural death was the least of my evils; for supposing I should escape with life by some strange adventure, how could I think with temper of passing my days among Yahoos?

After presenting him with my humble thanks for the offer of his servants' assistance in making a vessel, and desiring a reasonable time for so difficult a work, I told him I would endeavor to obey him.

My master in a few words made me a very gracious reply, allowed me the space of two months to finish my boat; and ordered the sorrel nag, my fellow servant (for so at this distance I may presume to call him), to follow my instructions, because I told my master that his help would be sufficient, and I knew he had a tenderness for me.

In his company my first business was to go to that part of the coast where my rebellious crew had ordered me to be set on shore. I got upon a height, and looking on every side into the sea, fancied I saw a small island toward the northeast. I took out my pocket glass, and could then clearly distinguish it about five leagues off, as I computed. But it appeared to the sorrel nag to be only a blue cloud; for as he had no conception of any country besides his own, so he could not be as expert in distinguishing remote objects at sea.

After I had discovered this island, I considered no further; but resolved it should, if possible, be the first place of my banishment, leaving the consequence to fortune.

I returned home, and consulting with the sorrel nag, we went into a copse at some distance, where I with my knife, and he with a sharp flint fastened very artificially after their manner to a wooden handle, cut down several oak wattles about the thickness of a walking staff, and some larger pieces.

In six weeks' time, with the help of the sorrel nag, who performed the parts that required most labor, I finished a sort of Indian canoe, but much larger, covering it with skins well stitched together with hempen threads of my own making. My sail was likewise composed of skins; and I likewise provided myself with four paddles. I laid in a stock of boiled flesh, of rabbits and fowls, and took with me two vessels, one filled with milk and the other with water.

I tried my canoe in a large pond near my master's house, and then corrected in it what was amiss;

stopping all the chinks with tallow, till I found it stanch and able to bear me and my freight. And when it was as complete as I could possibly make it, I had it drawn on a carriage very gently by Yahoos to the seaside, under the conduct of the sorrel nag and another servant.

When all was ready, and the day came for my departure, I took leave of my master and lady and the whole family, my eyes flowing with tears, and my heart quite sunk with grief. But his Honor, out of curiosity, and perhaps (if I may speak it without vanity) partly out of kindness, was determined to see me in my canoe, and got several of his neighboring friends to accompany him.

I was forced to wait above an hour for the tide, and then observing the wind very fortunately bearing toward the island to which I intended to steer my course, I took a second leave of my master; but as I was going to prostrate myself to kiss his hoof, he did me the honor to raise it gently to my mouth.

I paid my respects to the rest of the Houyhnhms in his Honor's company; then getting into my canoe, I pushed off.

I began this desperate voyage on February 15, 1714–15, at nine o'clock in the morning. The wind was very favorable; however, I made use at first only of my paddles. Then considering that I should soon be weary, and that the wind might chop about, I ventured to set up my little sail. Thus with the help of the tide I went at the rate of a league and a half an hour, as near as I could guess. My master and his friends continued on the shore till I was almost out of sight; and I often heard the sorrel nag (who always loved me) crying out, *Hnuy illa nyha majah Yahoo*: "Take care of thyself, gentle Yahoo."

My design was, if possible, to discover some small island uninhabited, yet sufficient by my labor to furnish me with the necessaries of life, so horrible was the idea I conceived of returning to live in the society and under the government of Yahoos. For in such a solitude as I desired I could at least enjoy my own thoughts, and reflect with delight on the virtues of the Houyhnhnms.

I resolved to steer my course eastward, hoping to reach the southwest coast of New Holland, and perhaps some such island as I desired, lying westward of it. By six in the evening I computed I had gone at least eighteen leagues, when I spied a very small island about half a league off, which I soon reached. It was nothing but a rock, with one creek, naturally arched by the force of tempests. Here I put in my canoe, and climbing up a part of the rock, I could plainly discover land to the east, extending from south to north.

I lay all night in my canoe, and repeating my voyage early in the morning, I arrived in seven hours to the southeast point of New Holland. This confirmed me in the opinion I have long entertained, that the maps and charts place this country at least three degrees more to the east than it really is.

I saw no inhabitants in the place where I landed, and being unarmed, I was afraid of venturing far into the country. I found some shellfish on the shore, and ate them raw, not daring to kindle a fire for fear of being discovered by the natives. I continued three days feeding on oysters and limpets, to save my own provisions; and I fortunately found a brook of excellent water, which gave me great relief.

On the fourth day, venturing out early a little too far, I saw twenty or thirty natives upon a height, not above five hundred yards from me. They were men, women, and children round a fire, as I could discover by the smoke. One of them spied me, and giving notice to the rest, five of them advanced toward me, leaving the women and children at the fire. I made what haste I could to the shore, and getting into my canoe, shoved off. The savages ran after me, and before I could get far enough into the sea, discharged an arrow, which wounded me deeply on the inside of my left knee (I shall carry the mark to my grave). I feared the arrow might be poisoned, and paddling out of the reach of their darts (being a calm day) I made a shift to suck the wound and dress it as well as I could.

I was at a loss what to do, for I durst not return to the same landing place, but stood to the north, and was forced to paddle; for the wind, though very gentle, was against me, blowing northwest. As I was looking about for a secure landing place, I saw a sail to the north-northeast, which appearing every minute more visible, I was in some doubt whether I should wait for them or no. But at last my detestation of the Yahoo race prevailed, and turning my canoe, I sailed and paddled together to the south, and got into the same creek from whence I set out in the morning, choosing rather to trust myself among these barbarians than live with European Yahoos. I drew up my canoe as close as I could to the shore and hid myself behind a stone by the little brook, which, as I have already said, was excellent water.

The ship came within half a league of this creek and sent her longboat with barrels to take in fresh water (for the place it seems was very well known), but I did not observe it till the boat was almost on shore, and it was too late to seek another hiding place. The seamen at their landing observed my canoe and, rummaging it all over, easily conjectured that the owner could not be far off. Four of them well armed searched every cranny and lurking hole, till at last they found me flat on my face behind the stone.

They gazed awhile in admiration at my strange
uncouth dress, my coat made of skins, my wooden-
soled shoes, and my furred stockings; from whence,
however, they concluded I was not a native of the
place, who all go naked. One of the seamen in Portuguese bid me rise, and asked who I was. I understood that language very well, and getting upon my
feet, said I was a poor Yahoo, banished from the Houyhnhnms, and desired they would please to let me
depart. They admired to hear me answer them in
their own tongue, and saw by my complexion I must
be a European, but were at a loss to know what I
meant by Yahoos and Houyhnhnms, and at the same
time fell a-laughing at my strange tone in speaking,
which resembled the neighing of a horse.

I trembled all the while between fear and hatred.
I again desired leave to depart, and was gently moving to my canoe; but they laid hold of me, desiring to
know what country I was of, whence I came, with
many other questions. I told them I was born in England, from whence I came about five years ago, and
then their country and ours were at peace. I therefore hoped they would not treat me as an enemy,
since I meant them no harm, but was a poor Yahoo,
seeking some desolate place where to pass the remainder of his unfortunate life.

When they began to talk, I thought I never heard
or saw anything so unnatural; for it appeared to me

as monstrous as if a dog or a cow should speak in England, or a Yahoo in Houyhnhnm-land. The honest Portuguese were equally amazed at my strange dress, and the odd manner of delivering my words, which however they understood very well. They spoke to me with great humanity, and said they were sure the captain would carry me gratis to Lisbon, from whence I might return to my own country. Two of the seamen would go back to the ship, inform the captain of what they had seen, and receive his order. In the meantime, unless I would give my solemn oath not to fly, they would secure me by force. I thought it best to comply with their proposal. They were very curious to know my story, but I gave them very little satisfaction; and they all conjectured that my misfortunes had impaired my reason.

In two hours the boat, which went laden with barrels of water, returned with the captain's command to fetch me on board. I fell on my knees to preserve my liberty; but all was in vain, and the men having tied me with cords, heaved me into the boat, from whence I was taken into the ship, and from thence into the captain's cabin.

His name was Pedro de Mendez and he was a very courteous and generous person. He entreated me to give some account of myself, and desired to know what I would eat or drink. He said I should be used as well as himself, and spoke so many obliging things

that I wondered to find such civilities from a Yahoo. However, I remained silent and sullen. I was ready to faint at the very smell of him and his men. At last I desired something to eat out of my own canoe; but he ordered me a chicken and some excellent wine, and then directed that I should be put to bed in a very clean cabin.

After dinner Don Pedro came to me and assured me he only meant to do me all the service he was able, and spoke so very movingly that at last I condescended to treat him like an animal which had some little portion of reason. I gave him a very short relation of my voyage, of the conspiracy against me by my own men, of the country where they set me on shore, and of my three years' residence there—all which he looked upon as if it were a dream or a vision. Whereat I took great offense, for I had quite forgotten the faculty of lying, so peculiar to Yahoos in all countries where they preside, and, consequently, the disposition of suspecting truth in others of their own species. I asked him whether it were the custom in his country to *say the thing that was not*. I assured him I had almost forgotten what he meant by falsehood, and if I had lived a thousand years in Houyhnhnm-land, I should never have heard a lie from the meanest servant.

The captain, a wise man, after many endeavors to catch me tripping in some part of my story, at last began to have a better opinion of my veracity, and the rather because he confessed he met with a Dutch skipper who pretended to have landed with five others of his crew upon a certain island or continent south of New Holland, where they went for fresh water, and observed a horse driving before him several animals exactly resembling those I described under the name of Yahoos. But he added that since I professed so inviolable an attachment to truth, I must give him my word of honor to bear him company in this voyage, without attempting anything against my life, or else he would continue me a prisoner till we arrived at Lisbon. I gave him the promise he required, but at the same time protested that I would suffer the greatest hardships rather than return to live among Yahoos.

Our voyage passed without any considerable accident. In gratitude to the captain I sometimes sat with him at his earnest request, and strove to conceal my antipathy to humankind, although it often broke out, which he suffered to pass without observation. But the greatest part of the day I confined myself to my cabin, to avoid seeing any of the crew.

We arrived at Lisbon, November 5, 1715. At our landing the captain forced me to cover myself with his cloak, to prevent the rabble from crowding about me. I was conveyed to his own house, and at my earnest request he led me up to the highest room backwards. I begged him to conceal from all persons what

I had told him of the Houyhnhnms, because the least hint of such a story would not only draw numbers of people to see me, but probably put me in danger of being imprisoned. The captain persuaded me to accept a suit of clothes newly made. I would not suffer the tailor to take my measure, but, since Don Pedro was almost of my size, they fitted me well enough. He outfitted me with other necessaries all new.

The captain had no wife, nor above three servants, none of which were suffered to attend at meals, and his whole deportment was so obliging, added to very good *human* understanding, that I really began to tolerate his company. He gained so far upon me that I ventured to look out of the back window. By degrees I was brought into another room, from whence I peeped into the street, but drew my head back in a fright. In a week's time he got me down to the door. I found my terror gradually lessened, but my hatred and contempt seemed to increase. I was at last bold enough to walk the street in his company.

In ten days Don Pedro, to whom I had given some account of my domestic affairs, put it upon me as a matter of honor and conscience that I ought to return to my native country and live at home with my wife and children. He told me there was an English ship in the port just ready to sail, and he would furnish me with all things necessary.

I complied at last, finding I could not do better. I

left Lisbon the 24th day of November, in an English merchantman, but who was the master I never inquired. Don Pedro accompanied me to the ship, and lent me twenty pounds. During this last voyage I had no commerce with the master or any of his men; but pretending I was sick, kept close in **my** cabin. On the 5th of December, 1715, we cast anchor in the Downs about nine in the morning, and at three in the afternoon I got safe to my house at Redriff.

My wife and family received me with great surprise and joy, because they had concluded me certainly dead. But I must freely confess the sight of them filled me only with hatred, disgust, and contempt, and the more by reflecting on the near alliance I had to them. For although since my unfortunate exile from the Houyhnhnm country I had compelled myself to tolerate the sight of Yahoos, and to converse with Don Pedro de Mendez, yet my memory and imagination were perpetually filled with the virtues and ideas of those exalted Houyhnhnms.

At the time I am writing it is five years since my last return to England: during the first year I could not endure my wife or children in my presence, much less could I suffer them to eat in the same room. To this hour they dare not presume to touch my bread, or drink out of the same cup, neither was I ever able to let one of them take me by the hand. The first money I laid out was to buy two young stallions, which I keep in a good stable, and next to them the groom is my greatest favorite. My horses understand me tolerably well. I converse with them at least four hours every day. They are strangers to bridle or saddle; they live in great amity with me, and friendship to each other.

Thus, gentle reader, I have given thee a faithful history of my travels for sixteen years and above seven months; wherein I have not been so studious of ornament as truth.

It is easy for us who travel into remote countries, which are seldom visited by Englishmen or other Europeans, to form descriptions of wonderful animals both at sea and land. Whereas a traveler's chief aim should be to make men wiser and better, and to improve their minds by the bad as well as good example of what they deliver concerning foreign places.

Having thus answered the only objection that can ever be raised against me as a traveler, I here take a final leave of all my courteous readers, and return to enjoy my own speculations in my little garden at Redriff; to apply those excellent lessons of virtue which I learned among the Houyhnhnms; to instruct the Yahoos of my own family as far as I shall find them docile animals; to behold my figure often in a glass, and thus if possible habituate myself by time to tolerate the sight of a human creature; to lament the brutality of Houyhnhnms in my own country, but always treat their persons with respect, for the sake of my noble master, his family, his friends, and the whole Houyhnhnm race, whom these of ours have the honor to resemble.

I began last week to permit my wife to sit at dinner with me, at the farthest end of a long table, and to answer (but with the utmost brevity) the few questions I ask her. And although it be hard for a man late in life to remove old habits, I am not altogether out of hopes in some time to suffer a neighbor Yahoo in my company, without the apprehensions I am yet under of his teeth or his claws.

THE BEAUTIFUL
Illustrated Junior Library
EDITIONS

378

Sw   Swift, Jonathan

Gulliver's travels

Sw   Swift, Jonathan

Gulliver's travels

DATE DUE	BORROWER'S NAME	ROOM NO.
APR 2 6 1978	Scott	
JAN 2 4	Chris M.	
JAN 2 5 1999		